The YEAR of
the STRANGER

To Douglas Young

The YEAR of the STRANGER

Allan Campbell McLean

CANONGATE KELPIES

First published 1971 by William Collins plc
First published in Kelpies 1994

Copyright © Allan Campbell McLean 1971
Cover illustration by Rob Fairley

British Library Cataloguing-in-Publication Data
A catalogue record for this book is available
on request from the British Library.

ISBN 0 86241 485 7

Printed and bound in Denmark by Nørhaven A/S

CANONGATE PRESS LTD, 14 FREDERICK STREET,
EDINBURGH EH2 2HB

My name is Calum Og, the son of Domhnull Ban, who was lost aboard a whaler out of Nantucket in the year 1865. My father came from the township of Glenuig in the Isle of Skye, and I believe he would have ended his days there, like his father before him — aye, and countless generations before them — if he had been left in peace to tend his cattle and crops. But on the very day that Mr Lincoln freed the slaves in America my father's homestead was unroofed by those with the law at their back, and because he resisted he had to take to the heather, a hunted outlaw with a price on his head.

Once he was gone from the place, the others went quietly. The thatch was stripped from their homes, their roofbeams cast down, their fires made black; and although the women wept the men made no move to resist, tight snared by those armed with important looking papers bearing the Sheriff's seal, demanding obedience to the law in a language they did not understand.

They were banished from the broad glen to cluster around the shore of the sea-loch far below, where the land was poor and one bad harvest meant famine for a twelvemonth. Thirty familes, deprived of their hill grazings, scratched for a living on the shore, and that was the year the herring shoals stayed clear of the loch, and were never seen again. The hill grazings, and all of Glenuig, were let to one man from the south — a brother of the factor — and sheep grazed among the ruins of the homes of the people.

Many's the time I have heard them tell of the great days when Glenuig and all the hill was ours; how at the start of summer they gathered their flocks and left the glen and made for the sheilings in the high grazings. The hills resounded with laughter the long summer through; the days spent in games and trials of strength, the nights in song and story around the fires under the light of the moon. I never knew the summer sheilings, or my father, and yet the memory of them — and him — is strong within me.

You need to know something of my father, and how it was with us in the old days, to understand my story. I have told how it all came to pass, how I was at Uamh an Oir *on that black October Sabbath — the thirteenth day of the month — in the year 1877, and it was given to me to witness the glory of the Cave of Gold.*

1

Something wet and cold hit me across the belly, jerking me awake, although in truth it was more like the start of a nightmare than an awakening. My eyes came open right enough, blinking against the fierce June sun, but my mind was that thick with sleep it was not in me to make a move.

I saw the big tackety boots, one on either side of me, the oiled thread of the treble stitching marching in trim lines across the toecaps; the homespun stockings clinging to the swelling calves; the tidy darn where a barb had made a jagged tear in the heavy tweed of the knickerbockers; the bursting neck tight cased in its stiff Sabbath collar; and I knew it was Fearghus Mor who had caught me, even before I took in his angry red moon of a face glaring down at me.

I lay still, clown that I was, thinking it might have been worse, thinking it might have been Mr Ferguson, the Head Keeper, a silent man from the south, whose stiff tongue was a stranger to the Gaelic, not that he had any need of the Gaelic seeing he could bring the rest of the keepers running — and Fearghus Mor was one of them — by the flick of a finger. Or it might have been the black terror of a factor himself, at whose word even Mr Ferguson was all humble obedience, as eager as any dog to spring to the command of his master.

I got another slash with the dripping wet branch of alder that Fearghus Mor gripped in his big fist, this time across the face. That stirred me. I scrambled out from under the arch of his legs, and got to my feet, brushing wet leaves from my smarting cheek and neck. My trousers and shirt were on the mossy bank between us. I snatched up my trousers and turned away from him, and pulled them on, awkward in my haste. He brought the alder branch down across my back with such a thwack that it flew out of his hand and slid down the bank into the river where it drifted away. I grabbed my shirt and held it bunched against my chest, afraid to pull it on for fear he would strike me with his fist as I drew it over my head.

The only sound was the murmuring flow of the river, the drone of bees busy working, the thin song of a lark high overhead — and Fearghus Mor's breathing. You would have thought there was a bellows on the go pumping air in and out of his lungs. The man was fit to burst by the look of him, and I knew fine why he was on the boil. If he gave tongue, he would roar at me, and it was the Sabbath day and in this place the Sabbath is the day for silence and the whispered word, the township sunk in a quiet near as deep as sleep; a quiet fit to chain the rage of any man, no matter how wild he might be. Not even Fearghus Mor dare roar on the Sabbath.

I do not know how long we stood there staring at each other, eyes locked fast; long enough I am telling you because I was wide awake by the time Fearghus Mor got himself in trim to speak. He put a hand up to his mouth and wiped the beaded sweat from his upper lip and spat at me through clenched teeth, 'What are you at, boy? Tell me that. What are you at?'

'Nothing,' I said.

If I had not been smart in ducking, the blow he struck at my head would have felled me senseless. 'I was drying myself just,' I added hastily. 'In the sun. I must have gone off to sleep.'

'Drying yourself?' he said, hunching the great spread of his shoulders, and raising his clenched fist again as he advanced on me.

'I was after taking a dip in the pool. It was that hot, I fancied a swim.'

Fearghus Mor looked across the river to the pool where a black hump of rock broke the green of the bank and marked the start of the narrow gorge. He shook his head, for all the world like a tormented bull trying to dislodge a troublesome fly that is biting deep. 'Swimming?' he said. 'In the pool? Are you wise, boy? The river is for the folk from the Lodge to fish and take their ease wi' picnics and the like, that has been the way of it since years. The river is for the private pleasure o' the gentry, and no wonder seeing it is costing the estate a fortune what with planting trees and fancy bushes galore and finding money for men's wages and the like and everyone knowing times is bad. Good grief, if word o' this trespass of yours should reach the factor there is no knowing what mischief would be done. Many's the one has been cleared from the place altogether for less. How would you fancy that, eh? — your uncle put from his croft, your mother along with him, and no door open for the three o' you save that of the poorhouse. For any favour, you are not wise, boy.'

'What way can the factor know?' I said hotly, 'supposing you are not after telling on me?'

I should have known that Fearghus Mor was not the man to let a thoughtless stab of anger go unheeded, but the words were out before I could choke them back. His temper came up like a pan of milk on a raging fire. Before I could dart out of his reach, his hand shot out and seized me by the upper arm, squeezing until the muscle was crushed in a numbing grip that had me squirming. He shook me as if I was of no more substance than a half empty bag of chaff, lifting me clean off the ground in his rage.

'You have a bold tongue on you, boy,' he growled, 'like your father before you, and you will come to the same bad end I would not wonder. You think I am for singing dumb and this place fairly crawling wi' folk that would go running to the factor with the least whisper supposing they thought it would put me in bad and profit themselves.' He glanced up the bare rock faces of the narrow gorge, and swung round to scan the ground downstream where the river twisted and turned through the green of the plantation, as if fearful of unseen eyes watching him. 'I am not so slow, boy, not me. Good jobs are not easy come by, and I am not for losing this one.'

'It would be hard lines if my uncle came to grief through me,' I said, the lie smarting worse within me than the slash across the face from the alder bough. 'And himself an elder of the kirk,' I added, giving time for the words to sink in.

Fearghus Mor did not speak, but he was thinking plenty, that was easy seen the way his whole body tensed and his grip on my arm slackened. Thinking did not come easy to Fearghus Mor, and he was working hard at it. I knew fine what was going through that mind of his. Everyone in the place said he was desperate keen to become a member of the Kirk Session, but you had to be an elder for that, and the elders were all for keeping their number few to make a bigger share of the power and the glory that was their rightful due. Fearghus Mor would be thinking that a good turn to my uncle merited a repayment, and what better return than the way being opened for him to take his seat as an elder at meetings of the Kirk Session.

He blinked — once, twice, thrice — like a sleeper slowly awakening, and his small, dull eyes were full of cunning as they regarded me. 'Maybe I will sing dumb,' he said, showing me his yellowing teeth in the nearest he could come to a smile, 'but I will tell you what you are needing and what I am going to give you. You are needing a right whipping, boy, and it is myself is the man to lay a stick across your back. When I am done, you will carry the mark of Fearghus Mor for many a long day.'

He let go of my arm and unbuttoned his jacket of good tweed, his eyes daring me to run for it. I was not so foolish as all that. He was fast on his feet for all his size, Fearghus Mor, and if there was to be a chase before the beating I was the one who would pay dear for it when it came to the laying on of the stick.

He had his jacket off one shoulder when a voice from the plantation downstream called, 'Nicolson!' And then again, curdling with impatience, 'Nicolson! Where are you, man?'

I do not know which of the two of us got the bigger scare. Me, I was done for when I heard Mr Ferguson's voice, expecting to see the Head Keeper stride out from the trees at any moment, and be pinned by his cold eyes, helpless as a rabbit in the grip of a stoat. But whatever the scare, Fearghus Mor was not slow in collecting his wits, I will say that for him. He tugged his jacket on to his shoulder, hissed, 'Hide yourself,' at me, and was off down the path as if he had been fired from a cannon, calling, 'Wait you, Mr Ferguson. Wait you, sir.'

He vanished into the trees where the river took a bend, and I was left alone, stupidly clutching my shirt to my bare chest, hopelessly trapped in the open as surely as if I had been staked to the ground for all to see. 'Hide yourself,' Fearghus Mor had said, but where? The path ended at the opening of the narrow gorge, the rock face rising sheer from the river. To the right, the ground was open, shelving gently to the hill, with clumps of sparse whin not fit to cover a rabbit and her young. The plantation was my only hope, but if I ran for the woods I might race straight into the arms of Mr Ferguson and the big fellow. I pulled on my shirt, more to break the trance that held me rooted fast than for any good it could do me. Shirt on my back or half naked, I was done for if the Head Keeper came on me.

I heard Fearghus Mor's voice, and the sound took me by the throat, squeezing what little hope remained clean out of my being. *There was a good run seeing the river was up after the rain last night. I saw three beauties in the lower pool.'*

There was a silence again, not the least sound, not even a twig cracking underfoot beneath Fearghus Mor's heavy tread. Then I heard his voice once more, booming loud above the steady murmur of the stream. *'There will be good fishing come Tuesday, sir, you can depend on that. The laird's cousin could not wish for better.'* His voice sounded even closer, or was he speaking louder to warn me of their approach? Like a cornered wild thing unable to stay still but finding every way of escape blocked, I took a few stumbling steps towards the gorge, stopped at the water's edge, and cursed myself for a fool; made off in the opposite direction for the shelter of a hummock of green, saw — too late — that the rise in the ground was not great enough to hide me; turned back to the river, and stopped dead in my tracks, knowing full well that I was trapped, my eyes rooted on the point where the path followed the bend in the river and entered the plantation — the point where the pair of them would emerge and see me.

A hoarse voice muttered, *'Thigibh an so,'* and again, like an echo, 'Come here.'

It was in me to believe that I had taken leave of my senses, for the voice seemed to come out of the ground. I glanced around wildly, desperate for the assurance that my eyes — if not my ears — were proof against deceit. Sure enough, I was the only one there, although my thudding heart was beating loud enough for two. I was in a bad way, hearing voices out of the ground, sweating that hard the shirt was stuck to my back, near eaten hollow by dread if the truth be told — and the worst yet to come, the Head Keeper to be faced, and maybe the factor himself before I was done.

I tried to break the shackles of fear. I told myself that was no way for the son of my father to be, craven and quaking with dread, and himself the one who had stood fast against the Sheriff Officer and his men, and never quailed. My word, he would not much fancy the sight of me, my father, if he could see me now — and that dismal thought, if you can believe such a thing, gave me courage.

Something clamped around my ankle, holding me fast.

My new-found courage was gone in the blink of an eye. As I am here, I swear my heart stopped beating. It was fear, and fear alone, that choked the rising cry in my throat, choked it dead. If I had not taken such a scare that cry would have been heard the length of the Ascrib Islands and distant Vaternish Point. 'Come quick,' the same hoarse voice said, 'or the keepers will be on us.'

2

I willed myself to look down. A lean, dark face — the face of a tinker, I knew that the moment I clapped eyes on him — lined with a rough grey stubble of beard, looked up at me from a hole in the ground. Only his head and shoulders and right arm were above ground. His thin brown hand had an iron grip on my ankle. I had a notion, foolish as it may seem, that I would have to carry that lean brown hand clamped to my ankle for all time to come. But even as the thought flitted through my mind he took his hand away, and scrambled out of the hole.

He was a small man, only an inch or two taller than me, but I had no time to get a right look at him, because he bundled me before him into the hole, which was as well seeing that the strength had gone from my legs and I could not have moved unaided. He dropped down beside me, and pointed to a stone-lined passage little more than the height of a birch-bough stool, and of no greater girth than a herring barrel. 'In you go,' he said. I got down on my knees, but before crawling into the underground passage I watched him swing a monster of a pivoted stone into place to close the opening. The stone was very near as big as himself, but he moved it with one hand, and it swung as free to the touch as the lid of the meal chest in our kitchen at home.

I had not crawled more than a yard or two into the pitch-black passage when my left hand slipped off something rounded that rattled against the stones. I stopped that sudden you would have thought there was a knife at my throat, tensed against I knew not what, hearing the muffled echo of the sound rolling along the passage. 'On you go,' the tinker said, as calm as you please, 'that was my pole you clattered.' I started forward again, feeling the pole against the heel of my hand. I counted eighteen short hand-strides before I was clear of it. That was some pole! But I was too fearful of what lay ahead in the dark to give much thought to what he was doing with a pole that length hidden underground. Mind you, if my wits had been working I would have tumbled to it right off, and I could only be thankful I was not fool enough to ask, and have him think me terrible slow on the uptake.

I stopped a second time on the long crawl through the underground passage, cramped and sore at the knees, suddenly yearning to make back and gain the freedom of the sun and air, not caring supposing the factor himself was waiting on the riverbank to greet me. The tinker grunted sharply at me to get moving, and I kept going after that, not wanting him to think I was afraid of the dark. By the time I saw a thin gleam of light ahead, the only thought in my mind was to find a place where I could straighten my back and stretch my cramped limbs.

The passage opened into a small chamber lit by the smoky flame of a *cruisgean* that sat in the centre of the floor. The flame flickered wildly, and made a mad dance, as I got stiffly to my feet and slowly straightened my aching back. Short as I am, my head cracked against the roof. I never felt the blow, I was that lost in wonderment.

The chamber was shaped like a beehive, and a snug bee-hive at that, paved and lined with large flagstones. Even the roof was of stone, long slabs resting on cross rafters. That was the biggest marvel of all to me, that the rafters themselves had been cut from stone. I could not take my eyes off them.

Half the floor of the chamber was deep in dry heather. The tinker sat down on the heather bed, and motioned me to do likewise. I dropped down, and stretched out, propped on one elbow, taking my ease on the sweet scented heather. That was when I saw the spear head. It was lying on the floor, glinting dully in the light of the lamp; a two-pronged spear head, spurred to prevent the salmon slipping free after she is struck. Likely, there would be another spear head fastened to the striking end of the long pole in the passage. I wondered how many salmon the tinker had grassed with his spear. Fearghus Mor would not be so cocky if he knew what lay beneath his feet.

I watched the tinker as he took a coil of thick black twist from a pocket of his ragged jacket, and sliced neat rings with quick, sure strokes of a thin-bladed knife. He ground the tobacco between his hands, and filled a short clay pipe, and lit it from the lamp. He drew greedily on the pipe, like a man taking food who has not seen a bite in days. Seated cross-legged on the bed of heather, in the dim light of the smoky *cruisgean*, he looked like a dark figure carved from stone. He seemed to have forgotten me, as he puffed at his pipe.

I gave a start when he said, 'How do they call you, boy?'

'I am Calum Og,' I said, 'the son of Domhnull Ban, the son of Calum Ban.'

'I am Mata,' he said, 'the son of Peadair.' He took the pipe from his mouth and spat. 'I am not needing a name on you to know you

7

for the son of Domhnull Ban. You are the dead spit of him, as sure as I am here.'

'My mother says no,' I said, hoping my voice did not betray me, for in all creation there was surely never another son who hated his mother the way I hated mine, and it was a secret I carried buried deep. 'She says it is her father I take after.'

'Ach, well, you need not look so down in the mouth,' he said. 'It is Domhnull Ban I see in you, and himself the one that will not be easy forgot in this place. Bards have made songs on him. The bard from Maligar made a great song on him.'

'The one about the Sheriff Officer?'

He nodded. 'Aye, that one. The song about Domhnull Ban sorting the Sheriff Officer.' He sat as silent and still as a graven image, then he sighed, and said, 'I doubt I will never see the like o' that again.'

'You saw it?'

'I saw it.'

'You were there yourself when they came?'

'I was there. It was the year of the big frost. There was ice on the river. *Dhia*, it was that bad the sea froze. It was — .'

'The first day of January, 1863,' I cut in, keen to boast that it was not in me to forget, wanting to show that I could roll the date off my tongue no bother, as indeed I could, and no wonder seeing the times I had heard it all in the hut of Seumas the shoemaker, as he worked at his bench and told the story time and time again. But Seumas had lived at the other end of the glen from my father. Seumas had not seen it happen, not with his own eyes.

'You have some memory, Calum Og, and you not born at the time,' he said slyly, and although no smile lightened his countenance, I knew fine he was laughing at me. 'The only bairn about Domhnull Ban's croft was a wee dark thing, not fair like you — a girl child, if I mind right.'

'Marsali, my sister,' I said, wondering why I did not take it on the nose, being laughed at by a tinker. 'June was come before I was born.'

'It was the year o' the big frost,' he went on, as if I had never interrupted him, 'and we were up on the high moor below Reieval. The living was bad. Empty cooking pots in the tents; empty bellies; the women without even the makings for a boiling o' tea. I made over to Domhnull Ban's for to beg a bite o' food and a poke o' dry tea — and maybe a fill of tobacco.' He took the pipe from his mouth, and examined it, fingering the bowl. Then he turned his dark eyes on me, and unless the flickering flame of the *cruisgean* was playing tricks I could have sworn there was a shyness at the back of the quick smile he gave me. 'I am a terrible man for the tobacco, Calum Og, terrible altogether, you have no idea. I can go without a bite for long enough, no bother, but I must have my smoke whatever.

'Domhnull Ban was good to me. I never went from his door empty handed. This day I had salt ling, girdle scones, a poke o' dry tea, and a fill for my pipe — aye, and tobacco for my pocket forby. Domhnull Ban walked me down to the green knoll — you know the place, *Cnoc an t-Sithein* — above the river. That was when we saw them, a right army making for the glen — the Sheriff Officer, two men along wi' him, and six big giants o' polismen at their back. It was the second coming o' the Sheriff Officer and his men. They had been out to the croft before at the back end of the old year, for to clear Domhnull Ban from the place, and he had driven them from his door with an old claymore that he kept hidden in the thatch.

'It is queer the way they go about it, clearing a man from his croft. You would need to be good at the book learning to rightly know the way of it. It is all done wi' bits o' paper. Once the Sheriff Officer has nailed his paper to the door, that is you done for, there is no more about it, you must go, and all them that has shelter under your roof. Even supposing your wife is with child, and your old mother lying badly in bed, and a wind from the north flinging snow in at the door, they must all up and go, if the Sheriff Officer has the right papers. It is writ on the papers. That is the law.

'Well, the Sheriff Officer waved his papers at Domhnull Ban, and said you are for out this time, my bold fellow, and what is more it is you for the jail seeing what happened the last time. Domhnull Ban never said a word. He just snatched the papers from the Sheriff Officer, and ripped them in pieces. Two of the polis made for him, and he felled the pair o' them. And before the rest knew what he was about he had seized the Sheriff Officer by the neck and thigh, and hoisted him above his head,' — Mata the tinker stretched his arms high, his hands upturned, fingers bent, to show how it was done — 'straight up, a clean lift, big an' all as the man was, and flung him straight in the river, right through the skin of ice. It was a cold dipping the Sheriff Officer had, I am telling you.

'*Dhia*, boy, it was pandemonium, you have no idea. The racket was enough to deafen you, cursing and swearing, I never heard the like. The Sheriff Officer's men made for the river for to rescue their master. Three of the polis had Domhnull Ban down, and a fourth was after trying to put chains on him. I cried that the Sheriff Officer was drowning, and that gave Domhnull Ban his chance. He got clear of them, and was away for the hill, running like a hare, and myself not slow behind him, and the polis behind me going for all they were worth. They were hardy, the polis, but they were not fit for the hill. We lost them before we reached the length of Bealach Uige. That was the night we slept in a cave above Loch Carcasgill, and near froze stiff. There was a wind coming down off o' Beinn Edra would ha' given the dead a fright.'

His pipe had gone out. He got it going again, and puffed in silence. Then he said, 'It was a long time ago, boy, the year o' the big frost, but I mind it like yesterday.'

'The Sheriff Officer,' I said, 'was he hurt bad?'

'Not him. He was still hungry for work when they hauled him from the river.'

'He put my mother out.'

'Aye, herself and the bairn, that very day. She was put from the house before the sun was down. And before the summer was spent every single one o' them — the best part o' thirty families — was cleared from Glenuig.'

'Were you long with my father on the hill?' I asked him.

'All that winter. He was all for making back down to the township, but we had word that his house was in ruins, the roof open to the sky. And his woman and bairn were safe with her brother. Besides, the place was swarming wi' polis, and there was a price on his head.'

'Did he ever see the glen again before he made off?'

'Once,' he said. 'The night before we got clear o' Skye in a fishing smack out of Staffin that took us the length o' Gairloch. We made down from the hill in the dark o' night to the croft of your uncle, the one wi' the bad eye on him. He was not pleased, the same one. It was a wonder to me Domhnull Ban got his nose inside the door. Mind you, it would have taken a bold man to stop him.'

'Did he say anything to you, my father?'

'How do you mean?'

'About going away.'

'To Gairloch? There was no choice, boy. It was that or the jail. The polis were on the prowl day and night. We had to get clear of the island.'

'No, to America.'

'To America? Aye, he spoke about America, right enough. When we were in Gairloch a man he knew from Culnacnoc said he would smuggle him aboard a fast barque bound for Glasgow. The night before she sailed Domhnull Ban told me he was going to make for America, and once he had got money he would be back for his family. He said this place was done, that the people would finish up on the shore eating limpets, if they did not stand fast for their land. He said there was land galore in America, and no lairds to take it from the people. He said if he could get a season or two at the whaling he would have money for land and many a thing forby. That is why he risked reaching down to the croft of your uncle before we left Skye, and the place thick wi' polis. He said his woman must know he was making for America, and would be back for her.'

'Was that all he said?'

'Aye, that was all — save for what he said to me.'

It was not my place to pry and poke for more, but I could not still my tongue. 'What did he say to you?' I asked, feeling the blood rush to my face as I heard myself speak, shamed by my nerve in asking a man to his face what he was not ready to give of his own accord.

The tinker took the pipe from his mouth, and buried it in his clasped hands. If he was not pleased, he hid it well. ' "I am no prophet, Mata, but we will meet again, supposing I have to cross seas to seek you out" — that is what Domhnull Ban said to me.' He unclasped his hands, and looked at his pipe. It had gone out. He stuffed it into his pocket. 'That was not to be the way of it. We shall never meet again, me and Domhnull Ban, not in this world.'

He got to his feet, quick and easy in his movements, for all the grey in his beard. 'The keepers will have made off,' he said. 'They are never long at the river on the Sabbath. You had best be going boy.'

I caught his arm, as he made to get down into the low passage. 'Mata,' I said, 'who made this place?'

'Who knows?' he said. 'A dark people, like me and my kind, not big at all, that is what the old men of the tribe say. They say the dark people had this land for themselves in olden times; that the hills and the glens, the lochs and the rivers were theirs to roam free. But they were not good at war, the little dark people, and big fair men — giants just — came over the sea from out of the north and put them to the sword. The little dark people made these places for to hide, that is what the old men of the tribe say. Who knows?' His thin brown hand stroked a curving stone where it arched into the roof of the chamber. 'I only know I never laid eyes on the man born of woman who could shape stone the like o' that.'

He never said a word on the long crawl through the underground passage, and he was still silent when he drew me to my feet and we stood together in the darkness under the great stone that shielded the opening. I could hear the murmur of the river as strong as if I had been lying on the bank with my face over the stream.

Mata gripped my arm hard. 'You must never tell of this place, Calum Og,' he said.

'Not me, I said, 'as I am before God.'

Sunlight flooded in, blinding me, as he worked the stone on its pivot. 'Go, then,' he said.

Now that the time had come, I did not want to leave him. 'I will see you again, Mata?'

'We are camped by the burn below Reieval,' he said. 'Come to my tent when the Sabbath is past and we will talk.'

'About your time on the hill with my father?'

'Aye, but go now.'

I clambered out of the hole, and the stone thudded down before I could turn and raise a hand to him. I looked down at the stone, no different from other great boulders that broke the green of the bank, set deep in the ground as if it had lain there untouched by man since the first day of creation; and it was in me to wonder if I had dreamed it all — dreamed of the underground passage, and the salmon spear, and the beehive chamber, and even Mata the tinker — as I slept in the hot sun by the river.

But Fearghus Mor was no dream, I knew that fine as I came through the door of my uncle's house. He was not there, the big fellow, and the kitchen was the way it always was on a Sabbath morning, my uncle, Tomas Caogach, at one end of the bench, the big Bible open by his side, so that he could snatch it up if a neighbour showed face; my mother at the other end, her hands tight folded in her lap. Neither of them spoke as I crossed the earthen floor to the birch-bough stool, but there was a something about the pair of them I did not fancy; a something brewing under the Sabbath quiet. I could feel it in my bones that Fearghus Mor had been and told on me.

3

Tomas Caogach's big bony hand reached out and closed the Bible. Everything about him was big and bony and awkward-looking; his hands, his feet, his long arms and legs, and most of all his face, all bony peaks and crags from the high forehead to the long chin; a face thrown out of true by the terrible squint in his right eye. He tried to hide the squint when there were folk around by tucking his neck down into his hunched shoulders, and keeping his head half turned away from them, eyes downcast. A stranger would have taken him for a humble man, shrinking from putting himself forward, but I knew better.

He got up and shut the door, and came back to his seat on the bench, never once looking at me. It was not like him to close the Bible long before it was time for us to make off to the kirk, and why should he shut the door on the sun and air, as if their was sickness in the house? I shot a glance at my mother. Her hands were clenched that tight in her lap the knuckles showed white. Her eyes were closed, but she was not sleeping, no fear. Her lips were moving. She was praying, that was a sure thing.

Tomas Caogach's head came up, and he faced me square on. It was not often he did that. His good left eye was fairly boring into me; the squint eye straying well wide of my left shoulder. I looked down at the tidy earthen floor, not able to face him out, knowing my gaze would be drawn to that wandering right eye of his, and I would be seized by a terrible urge to glance around and discover the object of its blind stare. It was queer the way the squint seemed to split his face clean in two. I always got the foolish notion that the two halves did not belong, that the wrong pieces had been matched, and that was why they made so ill-favoured a whole. It was always the same when I got to thinking like that, I could feel a nervous bubble of laughter rising in my throat. I swallowed it down, and sat still on the stool, watching a black beetle cross the floor.

'You were gone a terrible time putting out the cattle,' he said, in that soft voice of his that never rose above the same quiet drone no matter how wild he was. 'What was keeping you?'

'I took a walk,' I said, not able to remain still any longer, scraping at a leg of the stool with my thumbnail.

'So you took a walk,' he said, fairly purring, 'and it the

13

Sabbath. Who learned you that the Sabbath was the day for the taking o' idle jaunts? Not me, boy. Not your mother. Putting out cattle beasts to grass is a work o' necessity and mercy, sanctioned by the Most High. We have the word o' Holy Scriptures for that. Only the wicked would make mock o' the Sabbath by taking idle jaunts, and it is laid down in Holy Scriptures that the wicked shall be crowded like bricks in a fiery furnace. I am telling you, boy, you should be down on your knees quaking and trembling at the thought of the everlasting fire that awaits the wicked. What a bed is theirs to lie on; no straw to ease their bones, but fire; no friends, but furies; no sun to mark the passage o' time, but darkness — fire eternal, always burning, never dying away. Who can endure everlasting flame, boy? It shall not be quenched night or day, and the smoke from the burning will rise for ever and ever, though mountains crumble and seas go dry.' He had to stop for breath, but he was soon on the go again, thrusting his long nose forward, and saying, 'Where were you after walking, boy?'

I gave a shrug.

'Where were you walking, boy,' he repeated softly, 'and you gone so long.'

'Och, here and there,' I said.

'Here and there, was it? You hear him, Iseabal?' he said to my mother. 'He says he was walking here and there.'

My mother shot me a dagger of a look, but she did not speak. She was too well acquaint with the ways of her brother to venture a word out of turn.

'Here-and-There,' he said, running the words together, and making them sound like a strange name that had him puzzled. 'I never heard tell of a place called Here-and-There. Where is it, boy? Likely over the hill beyond the Maoladh Mor, seeing the time you were gone.'

'I was putting out the beasts,' I said sullenly.

'And taking an idle jaunt,' he said. 'Where did you go, boy?'

'I sat in the sun.'

'You hear him, Iseabal?' he said to my mother. 'He sat in the sun. Wait you, it is coming out. There will be more yet, I am telling you.' He sat forward, stroking his chin, his squint eye fixed full on the spinning wheel in the corner, his good eye latched firm on my face. 'Hear me, boy,' he said. 'Where were you sitting in the sun?'

'Amn't I after telling you?'

'No, I am waiting, and you the one to try the patience o' Job.'

'I was putting out the beasts.'

'Aye.'

'On the moor.'

'Well?'

'It was a great morning. The sun was blazing . . .'

'It was the Lord's Day.'

'. . . and I fancied sitting in the sun just.'

'Where?'

'Where do you think?'

'Watch your tongue boy. I am asking you — where?'

'Where else but the moor?' I said, not coming out with a straight untruth, but getting as near as I dared.

'Lies!' my mother shrieked. 'Lies! That tongue o' yours will be your undoing; it is a stranger to the truth, as sure as I am here.'

'Well, if he knows where I was, what is he asking me for?' I said to her, desperate for an end to the questioning. Anything was better than having him keep on at me.

She glanced at her brother, her mouth working, the tears starting to her eyes. But she had no need to struggle for words; one look at him was enough. He always had words in plenty ready fashioned dripping smooth from his tongue. 'Why am I asking you, boy?' he said. 'For to find the truth, so that justice can be done, and it not easy wi' you that full of sin.' He paused, and drew a heavy breath, and I knew what was coming before the words fell. 'It was not the moor you were on, but the laird's plantation above the road by the river, amn't I right? Sleeping, sprawled by the river, *naked!*'

'*A Chruitheachd!*' my mother cried. 'Naked! And it the Sabbath!' She started to sob.

'Naked as the day he was born,' Tomas Caogach affirmed, 'and that on the solemn word o' Fearghus Mor, and himself not the man for to be telling lies.'

There was a silence. I squirmed on the stool, more naked than I had ever been in the sun on the riverbank. Then the two of them started in on me, like a pair of hungry gulls tearing at a dead thing, each of them that eager to strike they were at it again before the one was right done, spewing the words that fast I was not sure who was saying what.

'Are you wise, boy?'

'Have you no thought of the shame of it?'

'You know fine it is eviction for trespass. That has been the way of it since years.'

15

'And your own sister in service at the Lodge. You think the factor would keep Marsali in her good job and her brother caught trespassing at the river? Never the day. She would be down the road in disgrace.'

'Not just trespass. You would ha' been charged wi' poaching, nothing surer, and the factor cannot abide poachers. Good grief, I believe that is why we were cleared from Glenuig; the factor was scunnered to death wi' the poaching that was going on, and no wonder. That father o' yours was never away from the river supposing he saw the least chance of lifting a salmon.'

'What if one o' the gentry had come on you lying naked?'

'And word got to the *Ceistear*, and me an elder o' the kirk.'

'You will be the death o' me yet, boy. I do not know what has got into you, and that is the truth of it.'

'The Devil himself, that is easy seen.'

'Is one in the family hunted by the police not enough?'

'No, this one is after taking the same road. Think o' the shame of his father, fleeing from the police, and making off to America without a word to the mother of his children. But this one is fit for worse before he is done. This one is that bold, he is without shame. Supposing he had his hand on the Holy Bible, the lies would slide off his tongue, and himself think nothing of it.'

That was Tomas Caogach laying off his chest, and shouting, too. It was not the shouting, strange as that was coming from him, but his words that brought me up off the birch-bough stool, as sharp as if a fire had been lighted under me.

'Lies, is it?' I was the one who was shouting now, and they were that taken aback they could only gape at me. 'You are the one making lies, saying my father went off to America without a word to her.' I pointed a trembling finger at my mother, but my eyes never left Tomas Caogach's face. 'You are the liar, as I am before God.'

What a rage consumed him! I thought he was going to take a fit. The colour flooded to his face, and ebbed every bit as quick, leaving the skin grey, waxed with sweat. A knotted vein in his forehead started to jump, and he screwed the palm of his hand into it, as if trying to press that throbbing vein into submission. But when he dropped his hand the vein was still pulsing strong, and his hand was shaking. His lips moved, but no sound issued. My mother was the first to get her tongue working. 'On your knees, boy,' she screamed, 'on your knees before your uncle — him that has fed you and clothed you and sheltered you all the

16

days of your life — and beg his forgiveness.'

'Not me,' I said, quaking inside for all my bold words, 'and him making lies on my father. I know fine my father never left Skye without a word to you. Mata told me. Mata was along with him. Mata was his friend.'

'That *ceard*!' Tomas Caogach put the word off his tongue as if he had tasted dung. 'That *tinker*!' His lip curled, and he spat on the earthen floor at my feet. A dribble of spittle clung to his chin; he brushed it away with an angry sweep of his hand. 'A fine friend for a man, a thieving tinker slinking from glen to glen begging a living off o' them that bend their back in honest toil. It would take the like o' your father to make a friend of a tinker, and of all that heathen breed I never laid eyes on one half so fly as that Mata. As well a mangy cur for a friend as that one.'

'He was a good friend to me,' I said hotly, 'seeing he hid me from the Head Keeper.'

The words were out before I could check my tongue, but I need not have worried. Tomas Caogach did not seem to be all that interested; indeed, he was calmer now, seemingly over the terrible rage that had possessed him. All he said was, 'Well, well, so Mata the tinker was at the river, eh?' And then, after a long, long pause, 'That one would find a corner to hide in a field o' bare stubble, if it came to the bit.'

He had gone quiet all of a sudden, calm as if he was sitting in the kirk listening to the *Ceistear* flaying the ungodly. My mother made to speak, but he motioned her to be quiet, and sat silent himself for long enough, chewing at his lip, deep in thought. 'You will have to make over to the kirk without me,' he said, at length, to my mother. 'Be sure this fellow puts on his good coat and cap.' And to me: 'I will need to fetch the *Ceistear* to see to you, boy. If any man can sort you, it is the *Ceistear*.'

He got up, and stopped at the door. 'If the brethren ask for me, Iseabal,' he said, 'tell them it is the Lord's work I am about.'

He went out without another word, pulling the door to behind him.

The kirk we attended was on the far side of the bay from our township, beyond the old burial ground on the bank of the Conon river where we carried our dead. The road came down from the high moor in the north, twisting and turning as it rounded the rocky crags, and opening into a long straight above our township, curving in front of the merchant's shop and the hut of Seumas the shoemaker. It took a steep dip before crossing the flat land of the bay, carried on stone bridges across the Rha and the Conon — the two streams that plunged down the hill and flowed into the loch on either side of the Lodge — and began its winding climb up the hill to the south.

Our kirk was perched on the side of the hill facing the great headland that guarded the bay from the north. The minister stayed in Snizort, and only came to us once a month, so it was Somhairle, the blind *Ceistear*, who took the service. They all said he had been a great fiddler in his young days, coaxing tunes from his fiddle fit to tickle the toes of the dead into a dance. But when he was nineteen Somhairle was stricken with the smallpox, and very near died. He lost his sight, poor man, although they make out he had not lost, but gained. He had seen the light, and was converted. When he rose from his bed, he smashed his fiddle in pieces, and went from township to township, preaching the word and converting sinners. They still tell of the day of the collection when he had all the folk from every township for miles around collect every musical instrument they could lay hands on — fiddles and bagpipes and concertinas and melodeons — and take them to a great gathering on the hill. When darkness fell, a bonfire of driftwood was lit, and every man filed past and threw his instrument on the fire. As the melodeons and concertinas and bagpipes and fiddles burned, Somhairle preached the word, and many a man wept and shouted he was saved, and women swooned clean out of their senses, and lay stretched out flat on the grass, waiting to be carried home when the last sinner had repented and the meeting came to an end. All that was long ago. Somhairle was well up in years now, spare and frail and plagued with the rheumatism. Only his voice was unchanged, they said — a great booming voice fit for a man twice his size — and his zeal in bringing sinners to repentance.

But it was not the blind *Ceistear's* voice booming loud in my ears that had me worried, or the times when his sightless eyes seemed to be singling me out from the rest of the congregation: it was the absence of Tomas Caogach from the kirk. When the precentor rose to lead us in the first psalm, I had taken a quick glance around, thinking he might have deemed it seemly to stay at the back, if he had been late in arriving. But there was no sign of him. And whenever my mother started to doze through the long sermon, I sneaked a look over my shoulder, willing for once to meet the full glare of his disapproval. But he was not there.

I worried myself sick wondering what had become of him. Tomas Caogach was not the man to miss public worship. You would need to chain him to a wall — and a strong wall at that — to keep him away from the kirk on the Sabbath. Long before I went to the school, he had me at my catechism every day in life, and I had to be word perfect on Question 60.

'How is the Sabbath to be sanctified?'

'The Sabbath is to be sanctified by a holy resting all that day, even from such worldly employments and recreations as are lawful on other days; and spending the whole time in the public and private exercises of God's worship, except so much as is to be taken up in the works of necessity and mercy.'

What work of necessity and mercy could Tomas Caogach have undertaken? None that I knew of. But there had to be one — of a terrible strong necessity and mercy — to keep him away from the kirk, and himself an elder. I thought about it until my head ached, but I was no wiser, not until we had made down the hill from the kirk, and rounded the bend by the tacksman's big house. Those in front of us had stopped, close-gathered by the bridge over the Rha, gazing down into the gorge below. I ran to join them, heedless of my mother's cry that it was the Sabbath and I must not run.

There was a procession toiling up the path from the gorge, led by Mr Ferguson and Tomas Caogach, the two of them shoulder to shoulder, and my uncle fine pleased to be at the front with the Head Keeper, that was easy seen the way he held his head high. Behind them came Fearghus Mor, leading Mata the tinker, yoked like a dumb cattle beast by a rope around the neck, his hands tied behind his back. Another keeper followed him, and a stableman from the Lodge, with a sack slung over his shoulder.

I got a better sight of Mata as he mounted the stile over the stone dyke above the road. His black hair was plastered wetly to his head, close as the coat of a seal, and his ragged jacket and trousers, the threadbare cloth black with water, clung to his spare frame. He had a jagged cut across his forehead above his right eye, the blood smearing his face from eye to chin, as it oozed from the wound. He may have been thin, Mata, but his blood was thick enough by the look of it. Fearghus Mor gave a sudden tug on the rope, hoping to bring the tinker crashing down — that was plain to be seen by the sly smirk he had on his big stupid face — but Mata leapt down from the stile as easy balanced as a cat. He never looked to his right or his left, as he was led across the road

19

and through the open gates of the Lodge. I was sure he had not seen me, and I was thankful for that.

The procession went on down the curving, tree-lined drive; the stableman, who had been slow in mounting the stile, hurrying to catch up. There were fish scales clinging to the sack he carried. I watched until the trees hid them from view, wondering where Mata found the nerve to show so little fear, marvelling at the way he had withdrawn into himself, so that he appeared to be indifferent to the cords that bound his wrists, aloof from the shame of being dragged like a roped beast before the gaze of the curious — some of them, like me, with not a quarter of his years to their name — as if he did not see them at all.

It is queer the notions you get, and it came to me that a person sees with more than his eyes. My eyes had been glued to Mata's face, and the faces of those who had captured him, but now that they were gone what remained with me, sharp in my mind, was the picture of Mr Ferguson's heavy studded shoes and Mata's bare feet, unprotected among the clattering tackets of the well shod, padding silent as the tread of a cat.

My mother came up on me from behind, catching me unawares. The crowd had drifted off, buzzing strong with talk for all that it was the Sabbath. She must have waited for them to be gone, so that she could give me a right lecture. She seized my arm in a fierce grip, and hung on tight when I tried to shake myself free. 'That is you done wi' running, boy,' she said, strengthening her grip. 'What way is that to be going on, and it the Lord's Day.'

Imagine! All she had in her head was me running a few yards to the bridge, and for all she knew her brother could have been lying dead at the bottom of the gorge. I was that sick I let her keep a hold of me, and she must have taken it for obedience to her will, thinking I had got a bad scare at the sight of poor Mata bound and roped. 'You look as if you are near weeping, boy, and no wonder,' she said, as we topped the brae by Seumas the shoemaker's hut, and turned off the road on the path leading to the croft. 'Let that be a lesson to you. You have Fearghus Mor and your uncle to thank that it was not you dragged before the factor accused o' poaching on the Sabbath.'

She could have been chattering away in a heathen tongue for all her words meant to me. I was thinking of Mata, right enough, and looking down in the mouth in all conscience, but my misery was caused by the thought of Mata believing he had been betrayed by the son of Domhnull Ban. There was only one cure for that. I must set him free before he was taken to the jail. It was not just me alone. There was Marsali at the Lodge, and all his tribe, camped by the burn below Reieval. I would not want for willing helpers, once I got word to them.

4

I never got clear of the house after the kirk. Alasdair Ruadh, thinking he was doing me a favour, brought our cattle down from the moor along with his own, so I had no excuse to be gone. The only break I got was the feeding of the calves, after my mother had done the milking. Then it was back to the house and the birch-bough stool, the big Bible on my knee, and reading aloud to her the words of the Preacher.

It was the only time I ever saw her at peace, when she had me reading to her from the Book. In a way, the Sabbath came badly to her, for she could not abide being idle. And all she could put her hand to on the Lord's Day was the milking of the four cows. Inside the house, her wheel was still; her knitting pins shut away in her workbox; water from the well, and peats from the stack, carried in the night before, when potatoes were boiled, porridge prepared, and dry tea placed ready in the pot, so there would be no breaking of the Sabbath. With her hands idle, she was in misery. She was forever plucking at her hair, and poking at stray wisps that had come adrift from the bun, or darting nervous glances around at the least sound, looking that fearful you would have thought she was certain sure the noise was that of a messenger at the door bearing bad news. But when I was reading from the Book she sat like one in a trance, hands limp in her lap, eyes rapt on my face. She could not read herself, and I believe she never tired of watching me spinning words from the black print that had always been a mystery to her, even though she knew the most of the Bible by heart. Whatever the reason, it stilled her tongue, and that meant there was peace in the house — until Tomas Caogach showed face and started in on me again.

But when he strode into the kitchen, and it long after we had taken supper — after a long wait before my mother could bring herself to serve food and him not there — he was in a good mood for a wonder. Indeed, he was in his glory, looking as near content as he would ever be in this world. He did not cast so much as a glance at me, that pleased with himself he could not see beyond the close glow of his own well-being.

He sat down on the bench, and ran a finger round the inside of his stiff white collar, stretching his neck like one of the tacksman's turkeys. It always puzzled me why he did that, as if

22

the collar was paining him, when in truth you could have put your fist down the gap between the circling collar and his scrawny neck. Maybe he did it just to remind himself that he had a good stiff collar at his throat — split new from the pedlar's pack — which was more than many a one in the place could manage. He was terrible vain about worldly possessions, Tomas Caogach, for an elder of the kirk. Even his house was different from the houses of the other crofters in our township. Whereas they had all built in the old style, the byre and living quarters together under the one roof, only a partition of driftwood separating the cattle beasts from the people, he had to go one better. His house had a kitchen and two rooms, the byre standing apart under its own roof.

'Mr Ferguson was fine pleased,' he said to my mother. 'Nothing would do but I must go back to the house with him and take tea. The man would not take no for an answer. And him that easy! You would never think he was after rubbing shoulders wi' the factor and the gentry near every day in life, and himself knowing Lords and Ladies galore — there is hardly a one he could not give you their pedigrees right off, back to their great-grandfathers at the very least, and all their titles and the like. But a homely enough man. Just like one of ourselves. And the wife, too. She was asking kindly for you was Mistress Ferguson. And you should have seen the tea she laid, Iseabal! Fit for a lord just! We were sat in at a table spread with a linen cloth white as a fresh clipped sheep. And food! I never saw the like. A whole ham; a big round o' beef; plates o' cheeses; baker's bread; oatcakes and scones galore; jams and jellies — I can't mind the half of it, the table was that loaded. He is a proper gentleman, Mr Ferguson, a proper gentleman. You will never guess what he was after making me take when I was for off.' He patted his pocket. 'A present o' tobacco. And all because I was not for a fill o' my pipe after supper. When I got up to go, Mr Ferguson said, "If you are not for having a pipe on the Sabbath, you must take tobacco home with you as a present from me."' He patted his pocket again, near stroking the cloth. 'A right handsome present it is. Oh, he is a gentleman, Mr Ferguson. If they were all like him in the Established Church, the place would be the better for it.'

It was changed days. Many's the time I had heard him miscalling the Head Keeper, saying he only went to the Established Church because it was no more than a dozen steps from his door, and himself too idle to climb the brae to the Free Kirk where we worshipped.

'What like is the house inside?' my mother wanted to know.

'What they call in English "well-appointed",' Tomas Caogach said, his tongue stiff to the English word, but speaking as if he had spent all his days poking his nose in and out of palaces and the houses of the gentry, and could sort them out the way the rest of us could tell a fresh run salmon from a kelt. 'It doesn't come near the Lodge, mind, nowhere near, but it is well-appointed right enough.'

I wondered what 'well-appointed' meant. Likely, he did not know himself, and had heard Mr Ferguson use the word. Maybe Mr Ferguson had said 'well-appointed', meaning the gaps between the stones had been filled well with mortar, and Tomas Caogach had got it wrong. I felt the laughter rising in my throat, and crouched lower on the stool, my hand clasped tight over my mouth, for fear a tell-tale gurgle would betray me. I gave a start when I realised that he had turned his attention to me, but he had not noticed anything amiss.

'You have got Fearghus Mor and me to thank,' he was saying, echoing the words of my mother earlier in the day, 'for keeping you clear o' trouble. It is as well some of us are not as slow on the uptake as you, boy. Were you after thinking the tinker was at the river for to sun himself just? The minute you put his name off your tongue I thought to myself that rascal Mata would think nothing o' breaking the Sabbath and poaching the river when everyone in the place, by his way of it, is safe gathered for worship, and there is not an eye abroad to see him about his work.'

He turned back to my mother, not wanting to waste words on me, that puffed up with himself he was bursting to tell her how he had trapped poor Mata, and earned the Head Keeper's praise and a present of tobacco. 'So I got hold o' Fearghus Mor,' he said proudly, 'and we went to Mr Ferguson, although Fearghus was not keen on the idea, and told him we had caught a sight of a tinker making down from the hill to the river. Mr Ferguson was not believing us. He said there was not a tinker living would dare, they were that fear'd o' the factor, and that ignorant, too, thinking the old law was still on the go and they would be transported across the seas to Van Diemen's Land for lifting a salmon. But he is not the man to be slack in his work, Mr Ferguson, and he summoned Colla the keeper and Aonghas the stableman, and the five of us bided our time until both kirks were in, and not a living soul was on the move.

'Well, well, Iseabal, you should have seen Mr Ferguson's face when we crept through the trees and came on the tinker. There he was, as bold as you please, busy with his spear. Aye, spearing salmon he was, and five beauties grassed on the bank to show he had not been idle. But he has some ears on him, that Mata. Before we got close enough to get a hold of him, he was straight into the pool and across to the north bank, and away like a hare, old and all as he is. He reached the length o' the Rha, below the falls, before we collared him, and if he had not slipped and stunned himself on a rock I believe the same one would be running still.'

'A mercy you got him,' my mother said, when she was done tut-tutting. 'The factor is the one to sort the like o' that trash. The factor will see to it that he is packed off to the jail, and put safe behind bars.'

Tomas Caogach raised a hand, holding her in a greedy silence. By the look of him, he had a tasty bite hooked close to his tongue, and he was not for giving her a chew on it without a wait to sharpen her appetite. 'The factor is away from home,' he said, at length, letting the words come out slow. 'But we have got the tinker fastened secure, never fear. Wait you,' he went on, as she made to speak, 'you have not heard the best of it yet. The factor is away for to take home the laird's cousin. And Mr Ferguson has been told to expect the laird's cousin out on the river wi' a rod come Tuesday.' He leaned back, and brought his hand down on his knee with a heavy slap, fair delighted with himself. 'I am telling you, Iseabal, the factor will go mad when he hears the river has been poached, and the laird's cousin home for the fishing. The jail did you say? The bold Sabbath breaker will be lucky if he ever claps eyes on the jail by the time the factor is done with him. You mark my words, the factor will have the skin off that tinker's back.'

His cold left eye swivelled round and fastened on me. I saw his lip curl. 'What ails you, boy?' he said. 'It is a wonder to me to see you sitting quiet on your stool, meek as a girl. Have you no word for your great friend, Mata the tinker? Or is it you fear'd, thinking you could ha' been the one locked up, awaiting the return o' the factor?'

'Calum Og has got a scare he will not be forgetting in a hurry,' my mother crowed. 'You should have seen the face on him when he clapped eyes on you making for the Lodge with the tinker.'

'He was badly needing a scare, stupid clown that he is,' Tomas Caogach said sharply, his good humour gone entire, speaking as if I were not there at all, as if I was as bereft of ears and feelings as the dead wood of the stool that bore me. 'Fearghus Mor was saying I have been too soft altogether wi' that boy. Fearghus was saying if he had the keeping of him he would take a stick regular to his back, and beat sense into him.'

As he spoke, his gaze kept straying to his hazel switch hooked over the back of the bench close to his right hand. I knew all about the wicked cut of that switch; I had felt it often enough, no matter how soft he made himself out to be. That was him all over, seeking the authority of another as the justification for his act. I knew fine he liked laying into me with the switch, but he was a great one for making out he did not much fancy that which he liked most. I closed my eyes, and prayed it was his squint that was deceiving me, because he had never beaten me before on the Sabbath. When I opened my eyes again, he was picking up the big Bible.

That was me safe. He was going to read a chapter, then we would get down on our knees, the three of us together at the bench, and he would make a last prayer before bed.

I lay snug in my box-bed in the sleeping corner of the kitchen, waiting until it was safe to make a move. That was the time I liked best, shut away on my own behind the blanket curtain, stretched flat on the pallet of clean straw, the wooden back of the box-bed — following the angle of the roof — rising close to my face, so that when I was of an age for such fancies I used to call the bed my cabin, and pretend that I was the master of a whaler searching the Southern Ocean for the great whale. It was best of all in the winter-time, the wooden back great for keeping out cold draughts and the drops of rain that always managed to drip through the thatch.

I lay on my back, and thought about my sister, Marsali. It was the last day of June, so she was fifteen years, four months, and twenty-seven days old — almost to the hour, because our mother said she had been born late at night. I did a bit more arithmetic in my head. That made her one year, three months and five days older than me. Not much of a gap between us — fifteen months just. But in some ways, she was very near fifteen years older than me, Marsali. She always looked as if she knew far more than she said, when it is the other way around with everyone else I know of our age. She had been working at the Lodge since she was thirteen, and that may have had something to do with it, for she never missed a thing, and there was plenty to take in at the Lodge, what with the doings of the gentry, and them talking that free you would have thought — Marsali said — they believed servants to be born without ears. Mind you, there was more to it than that. I had enough of her in me to know that what made Marsali Marsali came from within her, and not from any education she had gained in watching the gentry at the Lodge.

We were as different in looks as brother and sister could be — Marsali as dark as I was fair — but she was far away the best friend I had, not like a girl at all; the only person I could tell everything to, and hear from her things she would never let on to a single girl in the place. I suppose she took after our mother in looks, but where the *cailleach's* hair was a dull grey, caught up in a wispy bun that seemed to have throttled the life out of it, Marsali's was black as a raven's wing, fairly crackling with life, even when she had it tight threaded in a thick pleat. And whereas our mother's eyes were heavy shadowed, brooding deep — the very core of the sour look that pulled all the lines of her face down the way — Marsali's laughing eyes had you believing she was smiling when no such thought was in her mind. I often wondered if our mother had looked like Marsali when she was a girl, but one sour look from her and that fanciful notion withered and died.

We were different, too, in the way she could keep out of trouble. I never heard Tomas Caogach say a cross word to Marsali, and our mother never lifted a hand to her. The truth was the pair of them had no idea what went on in her mind, and if they had known they would not have believed it of her. Tomas Caogach doted on her. But he had never come on her making mock of him. She could take him off something wonderful, mimicking him to the life, so that all you had to do was close your eyes, and it was Tomas Caogach, laying off his chest good style — until Marsali collapsed in fits of laughter.

Tomas Caogach's long, rumbling snore broke into my thoughts, souding that loud through the driftwood partition I could have believed he was in the room with me. I listened until he was going at it steady before I got out of bed and pulled on my trousers. There was no sound from my mother in the other room, but she was a quiet sleeper, and not the one to stir before morning. It was dark in the kitchen with the outside door shut, the one small window, set deep in the double wall of unhewn stone, not big enough to lighten the room, and the fire, blackened by damp peats to keep it smouldering slow through the night, no help at all. But it would be bright enough outside. The day had only just begun to shorten, and in our island there is no real night in the month of June, only a short twilight before it is day again. I groped my way slowly to the door, and raised the latch, and eased it open. It was darker than I had thought. A great bank of white fog had rolled in from the sea, blanketing the loch, and starting to smoke up the croft. That was another hot day on the way, for sure. I slipped outside, and closed the door gently behind me.

There was a heavy dew, the grass soaking wet, chill to my bare feet. I ran up the bank to the path at the back of the house, and along the path to the main road. I left the road on its long climb to the crags, and took a short-cut, a narrow sheep track that wound above the old stone quarry, and twisted steep up the face of the hill. Up on the high moor, the air was colder, and I was glad of its cool touch on my sweating face. I climbed the drystone dyke that marked the boundary of our township's grazings on the moor, and stopped for breath, leaning against the wall. The northern sky was thick with haze, not a star to be seen. I looked back the way I had come. The bay was lost in white, only the tops of the twin headlands towering clear of the fogbank.

I set off at a trot over the moor, splashing through streams and patches of sphagnum moss, stumbling over tussocks of grass and heather, less keen on the task ahead with every step I took. I stopped again when I reached the hill road that crossed the moor and made down into Staffin by the rock pass under the Quirang, looking around to get my bearings. The moor was cut by the black faces of our township's peat bogs. I got a fright, thinking a man crouched watching me from the back of our own bog, but it was only the blackened rock where lightning had once struck, looking strangely like a human shape in the gloom. I ran on until I came to the burn. Not far to go now. The tinkers were camped beyond the next dark rise in the ground.

I stopped and listened, trying to breathe deep to slow my thudding heart. In all my life, I had only once come near a tinker's camp at night. Me and Rob, the grandson of the shoemaker, had done it for a dare the Hallowe'en before last. We crept up in the dark until we had a good sight of them sitting over their fires, taking their ease, thinking they had the wide moor to themselves. The noise they were making was the queerest sound I had ever heard, like the shrill chatter of a great flock of starlings. If it was Gaelic they were talking, it was not like any Gaelic known to me.

But it was the racket they were making — the high-pitched shrilling of their talk — that had me gaping, hardly able to believe my ears, too amazed to be afraid any longer. Tinkers, the silent people, never saying a word unless spoken to first, moving as quiet as thieves in the night, even when the sun was high in the sky — and there they were chattering as shrill as birds, every single one of them, it seemed, giving tongue at the same time.

Until Rob let go a shriek of a sneeze!

The shrill chatter was cut off as if they had been struck dumb on the instant. Every single one of them. There was not a sound. The silence hurt my ears, if you can believe such a thing. I did not say a word to Rob, and he spoke no word to me, but we were on our feet as one, and we never stopped running until we were safe inside the lighted hut of his grandfather.

I thought of that winter night as I listened, but the only sound I heard was the faint murmur of the breeze in the grasses, and the distant hoot of a night bird. I started forward again, wondering how I would summon the nerve to enter a tent and waken a sleeper. I was still snawing at the problem as I came down on to the flat beside the burn. It was a good place for their camp. The road curved away to the east. A dark shoulder of rock rose to the north of the burn, sheltering the camp site. But there was not a tent to be seen, not one.

My foot sank into something soft and warm. I got down and felt around with my hands. It was the ashes of a dead fire. There were more of them, ringed in a wide circle. I was slow on the uptake, right enough. Even by the fast beat of my heart, long minutes must have ticked away before it came to me that I was too late with my news that Mata had been taken, and needed help. The little dark people were not so slow. They had known who had seized Mata. And they had folded their tents, and fled in the night.

5

It was back the way I had come, as empty of foolish notions as the waste of moor was bare of people; no young men of the tribe racing at my heels, as I had imagined, close-gathered in support, pledged to rescue Mata. I was on my own, with only one person to turn to, and she not much older than myself.

I ran all the way, tired and all as I was, keeping on past the track to our township. Indeed, I did not stop running until I reached the enclosing wall of the Lodge, and had to come to a halt. I rested there, head bent against the cold, damp stone, panting hard. Once I had got my breath back, I was up and over the wall quicker than it takes to tell.

The sea fog had thickened fast, a clammy wet blanket, deadening all sound, and robbing the air of movement. It was queer, though, the way it seemed to set the trees on the move. I was forever stopping short, as a dark trunk suddenly rose before my eyes where no tree had been only a heartbeat earlier. But I got my worst scare of all when I was jerked around by the left arm, and a great black monster loomed above me. It was as well that I was paralysed by fright, or I would have been striking out at the rhododendron bush the way a bairn, waking in a night terror, fights off his blanket. I did not know which was the more shameful: to be too feared to strike, or hitting out at a harmless bush. Wild with rage, I wrenched my arm free of the clutching branch, and felt my jersey tear. I moved on again, hands outstretched, feeling my way forward.

I blundered on to the drive, thankful to have found it in the fog, but afraid to strike out boldly along the road. When I did venture to move, it was as if I was tethered to the tidy line of the trim grass verge. To tell the truth, my mind was full of the old men's tales of the *sluagh*, the ghostly funeral procession of those about to die. The old men had it all off; the dates, and the places where it happened, and the names of those, made bold by a jar of whisky, who had laughed at the stories of the *sluagh*, and footed it out for home in the dead of night, striding carefree in the middle of the road. And the old men told how the bold ones had met the silent procession of the ghostly dead that no force on earth could halt, and had been trampled underfoot, and found the next morning, crushed and broken under the tread of hundreds of feet.

I told myself you could not call the drive to the Lodge a right road, but I was not taking any chances. A right road or no, it seemed a right enough place for the *sluagh* to be on the prowl, what with overhanging branches drooping low like dead arms eager to get a touch of the living, so I kept tight to the grass verge. If I met the ghostly procession, they would have room and plenty to pass.

When the drive started to take a loop, I knew I was nearly there, although the house was hidden in the sea fog. The Lodge stood facing the sea, and the drive swept around the house to the big stone porch at the front. There was only the width of the drive between the porch and the low sea wall; at high tide it would not have needed much of a throw to toss a pebble from the front rooms of the Lodge straight into the sea.

I groped my way through the bushes towards the back of the house, getting a fleeting glimpse of a jutting gable and the dark line of a sloping roof; the fog parting in places only to swirl back again thicker than ever. It was that thick I very near walked straight into the outer wall of the kitchen where it stuck out from the main body of the house.

The kitchen, pantry and storerooms were new compared to the rest of the Lodge, built on when the factor first came to the place, the year before I was born. Marsali slept in a room under the roof of the kitchen, handy for her work. She was the first servant up in the mornings, and it was her job to light the big cooking range.

I climbed up the downpipe at the corner, and nearly came to grief in my haste to clamber on to the steeply sloping roof. My knee slipped before I had secured a right hold, and I was left hanging by one hand from the guttering. I hauled myself up again, and this time I got my knee firmly wedged in the guttering before seeking another hand hold. The slates were wet and slippery. I crawled up them cautious as a competitor at the Games trying to climb the greasy pole. Up and up, inch by inch, until I could reach out and get a good grip on the raised lip of the skylight. The light was open wide, secured on the third hole of its iron arm. I dragged myself up, and put my face in the opening, and called softly, 'Marsali! It is me, Calum Og.'

She had some nerve on her, Marsali. If that had been me, summoned from my bed by a voice from the roof in the dead of night, I swear I would have leapt my own height in the air, at the very least. And it was not as if she was lying awake, and had recognised my voice the moment I spoke her name. She was sleeping, the same one, sleeping like a dead thing. I had to call her three times before she stirred; and a fourth time before she answered. But she did not cry out or shriek or swoon, as you would expect a girl to do. She said, 'Calum Og?' drowsily; and then, wide awake now, her voice anxious, 'What is it, Calum Og?'

'I have got to see you for a talk, Marsali,' I whispered. 'Outside.'

'Wait you,' she said. 'I will come down. Watch yourself getting off the roof, boy.'

There was the sound of bolts being drawn. The heavy back door of the kitchen gave a squeak as it opened. She was wearing a cape thrown about her shoulders over her nightclothes, her hair hanging loose down her back. She closed the door gently, and took me by the hand, and led me to the woodshed, that quick and light of step it was clear she knew the way blindfold. We sat down, side by side, on a big chopping block. Shut away from the chill damp of the sea fog, the sweet resiny smell of fresh cut logs all around, I told her everything that had happened from the time Fearghus Mor had caught me sleeping by the river. Everything, except the underground passage and the secret chamber of stone. That was not for me to tell, not even to Marsali.

She gave a giggle when I was done, and said, 'I wish I could have seen the *cailleach's* face when she heard you were lying there naked.'

'How else was I to get dry?' I said, stung that she should laugh, not wanting to be reminded of the look on our mother's face. Supposing I never saw the like of that look again for a twelve month, it would be too soon for me.

'Trust you to fall asleep,' she said. 'Were you not scared someone would come on you, and you there with not a stitch on?'

'How was I to know I would fall asleep?'

'Well, well, you have some nerve on you, Calum Og,' she said.

That was a good one, and me frozen stiff with fear, not knowing which way to turn, until the tinker came to my aid. It is queer the notions people get, even the ones closest to you. 'Where have they got Mata?' I asked her.

'In the old meal store.'

'Where is that?'

'Over by the kennels.'

'Close by the kennels?'

'Right alongside. The keepers use it for the dogs' food and gear and stuff.'

'How many dogs are there in the kennels?'

She thought for a moment. 'Five just now.'

'He is a fly one, that Mr Ferguson,' I said gloomily. 'The dogs will make a racket that could be heard a mile off if anyone goes near the old store.'

'If a stranger goes near,' she said.

'How do you mean?'

'The dogs would be quiet enough if it was someone they knew.'

'You mean they would not bark at you, Marsali?' I said, brightening.

'They know better.'

'Supposing I was along with you?'

'I could keep them quiet easy enough.'

'What like a place is it, the old meal store?'

I might as well have come right out with what was in my mind. Marsali was not the one to be slow on the uptake. 'As good as any jail,' she said quickly, 'or you may be sure Mr Ferguson would never have left your tinker there. It has walls on it fit for a castle. Samson himself would have been hard put to break down the door.'

'Is there not a window to the place?'

'Just slits in the walls, not the thickness of your arm, like in an old castle.'

'I must speak to him,' I said, desperate to clear myself with Mata, 'whatever else I must speak to him.'

Marsali got up from the big timber block, and felt for my hand.

I knew that the kennels stood within a ring of bushes well away from the Lodge on the Conon river side of the grounds, but I had never laid eyes on them myself. Mind you, I had heard enough about them from Marsali — and many a one besides, or I would not have been believing her. The kennels were built of the same fancy dressed stone as the Lodge itself, six trim little houses of good dressed stone for six dogs, each with a hatchway door leading into an iron-barred run. It was a wonder to me why the laird had put masons to work building fine houses for dogs, and then had bushes planted to hide them from view. But there is no knowing with the gentry; they have some queer ideas.

Marsali led me along a path that crossed the kitchen garden, took a sharp turn away from the Lodge, and wound through a barrier of close planted bushes. There was a low growl; an excited yelp; a half-strangled bark. 'Be quiet, you fools,' Marsali said sharply. 'Quiet, I tell you.'

I could see the dark outline of the kennels now, through the wreathing fog. They stood lower to the ground than I had imagined. There was a higher, darker shape to the left. 'That is it,' Marsali whispered, giving me a push in the back. 'Away you go, and be quick about it.'

I stumbled towards the old meal store, and felt my way along the wall to the door. I put my shoulder to the door, but it never gave an inch. At my back, I could hear Marsali talking softly to the dogs, calling them by name. 'Mata!' I ventured. 'Mata!' There was no sound from within. Silence. 'Mata!' I called again, a little louder this time. 'It is me, Calum Og.'

A voice reached me, muffled by the thickness of the walls and the door, seeming to come at me from above. I stretched on tiptoe, feeling above the low door. There was a narrow slit in the wall, just wide enough to take three fingers. 'How are you?' I said, not knowing what to say to him.

'Well enough.'

Now that I had an ear cocked to the slit in the wall above the door, there was no mistaking that hoarse voice. 'Are you bound still?' I asked him.

'No, they have no need o' cords on my wrists, not in this place.'

'Did they give you food?'

'Aye, bread and water. I am not complaining.'

'Mata,' I said, the words tumbling out in a rush, 'it was not me that told on you. I was praising you to my uncle for saving me from the keepers, and it was himself took the notion to go to Mr Ferguson and tell him you were after salmon on the river. But he never let on to me what he was about. And it was not me that told on you — not about the spear not anything.'

'Calum Og.'

'Aye.'

'The hidden place? Did you tell about the hidden place?'

'I never said a word, not a word, Mata, not to a living soul.'

'They must never know, the big ones.'

'They will never know from me, never ever from me.'

'I believe you, boy.'

'Mata,' I said, thinking he had better know the worst, 'all your folk are gone. I was up at the camp, and they have flitted, every single one o' them.'

'Good,' he said.

I was struck dumb by his reply. It took an excited whine from one of the dogs, silenced by Marsali's angry word of command, to awaken in me the need for haste, and get my tongue working again. 'What way can I get you clear,' I said, angry at him, 'and me on my own?'

'What way could you free me without putting chains on all my tribe?' he said. 'I am not worrying, boy. It is not the first time I have seen the inside o' the jail for lifting a salmon, and I never died a winter yet — jail or no jail. Does that uncle o' yours know you are here?'

'No fear. The same one is in his bed, snoring hard.'

'Who is the girl along wi' you?'

My word, he had some ears on him, Mata, if he had caught Marsali's whispered words. 'My sister,' I said. 'She is keeping the dogs quiet. They know her. She works at the Lodge.'

'You had best be going,' he said.

'Aye.'

'Calum Og?' he said, after a long silence, Marsali hissing at me to hurry.

'Aye.'

'You are not away yet?'

'Not yet.'

'Calum Og?'

'Aye.'

'Calum Og, I am wanting you to do me a turn.'

'Anything at all, Mata,' I said, 'supposing I am able.'

'Calum Og, they are after taking my tobacco from me, and my pipe, and my tin o' matches. I am missing the tobacco something terrible.'

'I will get you tobacco,' I said, not even stopping to think how. 'But I am not so sure about a pipe and — .'

'I am not needing a pipe, boy,' he cut in. 'They would smell the smoke and know someone had been at me. No, no, tobacco just. If I could get a chew on a plug o' tobacco that would do me fine. But watch yourself, boy. I am not wanting you in the jail beside me.'

'Aye, surely. Well, I am away, Mata, but I will be back to-morrow night with the tobacco.'

'Just enough for a chew, mind,' he said, and once again, 'Watch yourself. A safe going, Calum Og.'

Marsali said a last warning word to the dogs, and was on the move before I gained her side. She took me out of the ring of bushes by another path that brought us up against the boundary wall by the Conon river. The fog was heavier than ever over the water, muffling the sound of the river as it flowed strong to the sea.

Marsali said, 'What was it you were telling him you never said a word about?'

There were more than Mata with ears fit to hear the grass growing. 'That he was making the white whisky,' I lied. 'In a cave in the hills.'

It was a good lie, if there can be such a thing. Marsali swallowed it whole. 'It would be the end of the poor *truaghan* altogether,' she said, 'if the factor got word that he was busy at the whisky making as well as poaching the river.'

'Have you word o' the factor?'

'The coach is to be up to Portree tomorrow, meeting him off the steamer. Himself and the laird's cousin.'

'I wonder what like a man he is?'

'Not like any you ever saw before,' she said, laughter bubbling in her voice. 'The laird's cousin is a Lady Something-or-Other.'

'Why do you suppose the laird himself never comes home?'

'The laird has more homes than you have freckles on your nose,' she said. 'He cannot nurse them all like a broody hen on a clutch. They say he has an estate in Africa bigger than the whole of Skye.'

'Away!'

'It's right enough.'

'A pity he doesn't put away the factor to Africa, and let the savages get him.'

'The factor would not be slow in telling the laird he is among savages where he is,' she said sharply. 'Those who have no English are every bit as bad as heathen savages to the factor.'

I had never thought of it like that, and the laughter died in my throat. Marsali was right enough, that was easy seen. It was to be seen in the cold, hooded eyes of the factor, eyes that regarded us as if we were of less account than dumb cattle beasts. Indeed, he had more thought for cattle beasts than us. They could halt the progress of his coach, but not us. His coachman never slowed, if we were on the road. We were expected to leap smartly to the side, and snatch the bonnets from our heads in salute. The thought of Mata at the mercy of such a man gave me the shivers.

'I am for seeing Mata tomorrow night,' I said.

'With the factor back home?'

'He must sleep some time. I will leave it late.'

'You have taken a great notion to the old tinker.'

'He helped our father.'

'But what can we do to help him?'

'Supposing it was me locked up in the dark,' I said, 'I would be glad enough for a word from a friend.'

'I would want out,' she said.

'Could you not get a hold of the key to the old meal store?'

'Mr Ferguson has the key.'

'Trust him. But you will manage tomorrow night, Marsali?'

'I suppose. But you are not to climb the wall until all the lamps are out in the house. And that will be late enough with himself back home. Make straight for the woodshed. I will take over a bite o' food from the kitchen.'

'Fine, Marsali.'

'Watch yourself, Calum Og,' she said. 'There is more than the factor would come down on you heavy supposing you were caught helping the tinker.'

She gave me a wave, and turned on her heel, that easy in the going you would have thought it was day, and bright with sun. If she was afraid of walking back to the Lodge on her own in the dead of night you would not have known by the step on her. I waited long after she had vanished into the fog before I climbed the wall, and made for home.

Tomas Caogach was still at it, as I eased open the kitchen door, throwing off great shuddering snores fit to shake the wooden partition to the floor. I pulled off my trousers, and got into the box-bed, not caring a hoot for his snores, I was that pleased to be safely home.

I had almost drifted off to sleep when I remembered my promise to Mata. Who could I ask for a plug of tobacco? Seumas the shoemaker was not the one to grudge a chew to a prisoner of the factor, even if he was a tinker, and Seumas not too fond of the breed. I would ask him in the morning. No, no, not Seumas, who would never grudge the gift, not him. Let the one make the gift who was as sparing of his pipe as if it was gold he had burning to ashes in the bowl. That was the one to provide Mata with a chew. I smiled to myself in the dark. The first chance I got I would slice a piece from the coil of black twist in my uncle's tobacco tin.

Tomas Caogach would be the benefactor. It was the least he could do seeing he was the one who had betrayed Mata to the factor. I went to sleep happy, smiling at the thought.

6

They were on at me, the pair of them, before I was right out of
bed, their voices dinning away as I struggled into my trousers.
My mother was creating because I was slow in rising, laying off
her chest about the hard times she had endured in her young
days; first on the go in the morning, and the last to lay down her
head at night. Tomas Caogach was not needing a reason; the very
sight of me, I believe, was reason enough to start him off.

The coming of the brose to the table put a stop to him. He was
quick to bow his head for silence, and turn his tongue to the
saying of the grace, greedy to get his horn spoon working on the
big bowl of brose that was steaming under his nose. But my
mother was away again, once the prayer was finished, taking no
more than quick pecks at her food as she laid into me.

'The trouble wi' you, boy,' she said, 'is that you are not ap-
preciating the comforts you have, and the work that is done for
you. Many a one in this place has no more than an old meal bag
for to cover himself in bed, and plain water to bite on for his
breakfast. You are too well off, boy, that is your trouble. A good
blanket snug on your bed, clothes on your back that in my day
would have been shut away in the chest for wearing on the
Sabbath, and all the — .' She stopped short, and snatched at my
left wrist, holding up my arm for inspection.

'Good grief, that jersey not a twelvemonth off the knitting
pins, and the sleeve near torn to pieces. What are you playing at?
Is that the way to treat good clothes, and them not easy come by?
It is queer I never noticed that tear before.'

'Nor me,' I said.

'You! That will be the day, when you notice the like of a tear in
your sleeve. Supposing your jersey was hanging off your back in
ribbons, you would never be the one to notice. How did you tear
the sleeve?'

'I have no idea.'

'No idea? You hear him, Tomas? He says he has no idea. How
can you have no idea, clown that you are, and a tear in your
sleeve that big you could poke your great head through it? Well?
I am wanting to know, boy.'

'I have no idea,' I said.

She tut-tutted away, shaking her head until her wispy bun

came undone, and that made her wilder than ever. 'It is a good starving, that is what you are needing, boy,' she said, trying to twist loose ends of hair back into place. 'There would be less picking at your food then, I am telling you. A good starving would fairly sort you.'

On and on and on it went, her voice beating about my ears like a flail; and once Tomas Caogach had scraped his brose bowl clean, he joined in. Water for breakfast? I would have gladly exchanged my bowl of brose for one of water, if I could have taken the water in peace, and not had the two of them on at me all the time. But I stayed where I was, not making excuses to get out on the croft the way I usually did. I was waiting for Tomas Caogach to set about filling and lighting his first pipe of the day, knowing he would leave his tobacco tin on the kitchen table, where I could help myself the moment my mother's back was turned.

He was always terrible hungry for his first pipe of the working week after his Sabbath abstinence, Tomas Caogach, so he strung out the business of preparing the makings as long as he could, anxious to show — to himself, I reckon, as well as his sister and me — that he was not all that desperate for a smoke.

First of all, the pipe was produced, and laid on the table. Then he dug into his pocket again, and out came the tin of tobacco to join the pipe. After a while, his big fist closed around the tin, and he got it open and thrust his long nose under the lid. He could not keep the smirk off his face at the sight of the coil of thick black twist wedged tight in the tin, far and away the biggest I had ever seen there. That must be the present from Mr Ferguson. Well, he would never miss a piece off the end of that monster of a coil, I could be sure of that. I watched him take out his knife and set to work slicing rings off the coil, his mouth open, concentrating hard for fear the blade slipped. The carefully sliced rings were not the thickness of a fish scale. My word, the *Ceistear* might be dead against smoking, but he could never accuse Tomas Caogach of being heavy on the tobacco. Mr Ferguson's present would last him the best part of a twelvemonth, provided he did not lose his touch with a knife.

He ground the tobacco together in the quern of his hands, and filled his pipe, tracking down every shred that escaped the bowl and fell on the table. When he had got the pipe going, he went to the door, and stood looking out. It was the same every morning in life, that halt he made at the open door to take stock of the day before venturing out on the croft. But this morning was to be different. He ducked his head, right enough, about to step under the big stone lintel, then changed his mind, even as he took a step forward. He turned in mid stride, and came back to the table and scooped up his tobacco tin and thrust it into his pocket.

I gazed at the corner of the table where the tobacco tin had been, hardly able to believe my eyes. Supposing he clung tight to the tin after his second pipe of the day at dinner-time? That would leave me with just the one more chance. Tomas Caogach never allowed himself more than three pipes a day, excepting the Sabbath when he abstained entire.

My mother poked me in the back. 'Sitting dreaming never filled a meal chest yet,' she barked. 'Away to the byre, boy, and get the beasts put out.'

The next time I got a sight of the tobacco tin was when we stopped work for a bite of food — not a proper dinner, although the sun was well past the meridian; a piece of girdle scone and a cup of tea just — out in the heather at the back of our peat bog. The tin was straight into his pocket once he had filled his pipe, and we were bending our backs again the moment he was done smoking.

I never knew a job so dull as the first lifting of the peats. They lay flat, spread out in neat rows, half at the bottom of the bog, half along the top, where my mother and I — working turnabout to the thrust of Tomas Caogach's iron — had tossed them, wet and heavy, as they were sliced fresh from the bog. That had been weeks ago during a dry spell in May, and the wind and the sun had given the topsides of the peats a dry skin, so now they could be lifted without breaking.

We stacked them in little heaps, six to a stack — one peat upright in the centre of the pyramid, four sloping in to make a firm stand, and one flat across the top — the wet faces of the peats open to the weather. Once they were no longer lying flat — and the bottom of the bog a swamp — they would dry soon enough, given half decent weather. But you have no idea the labour there is in the lifting of a store of peats sufficient to see off a winter and spring, and the drying of a new season's supplies.

All the long afternoon and early evening, with the sun scorching down from a sky free of cloud, Tomas Caogach, my mother and I kept on at the job, until I felt that I would never be able to straighten my back again. That was the worst of it; you were bent low the whole time, and there was no straightening at all, not with Tomas Caogach's eye on you. And the wet bog seemed to throw back the glare of the sun like a glass, the black face of the peat cutting glistening, as if oiled with sweat.

We worked on and on, until the peats on their feet far outnumbered those lying flat, and only the bottom quarter of the long bog remained to be lifted. But it would be hours before the sun took his brief dip behind the Western Isles, and Tomas Caogach was not the one to turn for home as long as there was work to be done, and a blink of light in the sky for the doing of it.

I was wrong, for a wonder.

He straightened his back, and pulled out his big watch; peered at it, and cast a sour glance at the peats still to be lifted. 'We had best make off, Iseabal,' he muttered. 'The *Ceistear* said he would reach over to the house at the back of eight.'

'I will stay and lift the rest o' the peats,' I said.

'Not you,' my mother snapped.

'It is yourself that is needing the lift, boy,' Tomas Caogach said, 'out o' the bog of sin you are in.'

'Never fear,' my mother said, 'he will get a sharp enough lift from the *Ceistear*, or I am sore mistaken.'

I heard his stick tapping at the wall, as he felt his way around the house to the door. Neither of them went out to guide him in, although the pair of them were swift on their feet at the first sound of his stick on the wall. They knew better than offer him assistance, for the *Ceistear* would not have it that he was less able than the sighted in making his way about, and indeed he was not. He came tapping into the kitchen, feeling for the end of the bench with his stick, and standing fast once he had got his bearings; a small, spare man, dressed all in black, only the tip of his starched white collar showing under his high-buttoned coat; face uptilted, as if seeking the sun, sightless eyes narrowed like one straining to see into the far distance, his small head, under the big black hat, forever on the move, turning from side to side. I used to wonder why his head was never still, not realising that he was seeing with his ears, poor man, and was always straining to catch the least sound so that he could make out what was going on about him.

Tomas Caogach advanced and grasped his hand, holding it in a long clasp, and then it was the turn of my mother. The *Ceistear* hushed the pair of them as they gave thanks for his coming, and tapped his way along to the plumb centre of the bench, and sat down. He took off his big hard hat, and laid it down beside him. The hair of his head was white, like wool. 'The boy,' he said. 'Where is the boy?'

My mother pushed me forward, and I took his small soft hand in my own. He pulled me down on the bench beside him. Looking straight in the direction of Tomas Caogach, he said, 'Sit, Tomas,' and at my mother, 'Sit, Iseabal,' and then, clearing his throat the way he did when he was high above us in the pulpit at the kirk, 'Let us pray.'

The four of us got down on our knees in front of the bench, the *Ceistear's* knees cracking something terrible. He was bad with the rheumatics. Maybe that was why he was slow in starting, having first to purge himself of all selfish thoughts, and he was bound to be wondering why he was plagued with such a stiffness in his joints, and him only wanting the use of his legs to get around and take the word to others. A heavy silence hung about us, like no other silence I had ever known before; a hard silence, thick with dread, a bit like the breathless hush that follows a bad thunderclap, every living thing knowing there is worse to come, waiting for the lightning to rip open the sky.

He started soft, the *Ceistear*, searching for words and not finding them easy, speaking that low I could hardly make out what he was saying, speaking as the spirit moved him, and it was as if that spirit drew strength and sustenance from the air, because the words came faster as his voice grew stronger, no faltering now, the words pouring forth in spate, the great organ of his voice booming loud in my ears. The first time he spoke my name, I heard my mother give a gasp, and soon she was weeping, whether from joy or sorrow I knew not. I chanced a glance from under my clasped hands at the *Ceistear*. He still held his stick, even in prayer, his small, white hands opening and closing around it, as his voice rang out, mighty as a trumpet blast.

I thought we were there on our knees for the rest of the night, and that is the truth of it, but his voice gradually slowed, grew soft again, became that low I barely heard his whispered, 'Amen.' We still knelt, the four of us, long after he was done, as if that voice of his had worked its spell and held us in a trance, a trance that only he could break. Break it he did, clearing his throat, and letting out a sigh as he got to his feet. My mother was the last to rise from her knees, and seat herself on the bench again.

But that was not the end of it, no fear. We were no sooner seated on the bench than he started in on the questions; sharp questions, fired that fast I do not mind the half of them. He had questions, the *Ceistear*, that would have drawn sweat through the thick hide of a donkey. And all the time his stick was on the move, tapping away at the earthen floor. I got the foolish notion that if only I could summon the courage to snatch the stick from him, and break it in pieces, that would be him struck dumb.

'Which is the fifth commandment, boy?' he said, his stick tapping out the words, his right hand gripping my leg, as if he must have a feel of me to make sure the question was biting home.

'The fifth commandment is, Honour thy father and thy mother; that thy days may be long upon the land which the Lord thy God giveth thee.' Tomas Caogach had learned me well.

'Who is your father, boy?' he asked, and not stopping for a word from me, his stick rapping Tomas Caogach's big boots. 'This man is your father, him that has raised you all the days of your life, fed you, clothed you, put you to the school, raised you true in the fear o' the Lord.' The stick rapped out its message on my uncle's boots. 'This man has been father to you, even though you name him uncle.'

The *Ceistear's* hand sought my leg again. 'What is the duty which God requireth of man?'

It was a wonder to me why he asked since he had taken me through my Catechism often enough. 'The duty which God requireth of man,' I said, 'is obedience to his revealed will.'

'Aye, obedience!' The *Ceistear* snatched at that one word quicker than any hungry gull swooping down on a tasty bite. 'Your duty to God is obedience, and it is God's revealed will that you honour your father and your mother. But not you, boy. I am hearing obedience is not in you. That is a sin; a terrible sin. And every sin is deserving of God's wrath and curse, both in this life, and that which is to come. Are you not fear'd, boy? Is it the pains of hell you seek — the pains of hell for ever and ever and ever?'

My mother was weeping again, and I was near weeping myself, what with that great voice thundering at me, and those sightless eyes latched fast on my face. I looked down at the floor, fixing my gaze on his boots. He had the smallest feet on him that I had ever seen on a man; feet encased in little boots no bigger than a boy's. It was easier looking at his little boots than those dead eyes.

'What is the biggest barn you ever saw, boy?' he said, all of a sudden.

I was that taken aback, I had no reply.

'The barn o' the tacksman?' he wanted to know.

'No,' I said, finding my tongue, 'I have seen a bigger — the barn at Kingsburgh.'

'The barn at Kingsburgh,' he said slowly. 'Supposing that great barn was filled to the roof with grains o' corn. To the very roof, mind. And supposing a bird — one bird — should come once — just the once, mind — every thousand years, and fetch away one grain o' corn. Just the one grain o' corn, mind, and that just the once every thousand years. Hear me now, boy. One day — be it ever so long — one day that great barn would be empty; the grain would have come to an end.' His voice rose to a shout, and he roared at me, 'But the torments of hell have no end. Ten thousand times ten million o' days are as the blink of an eye in the torments of the damned. Are you for chancing the like o' that, boy? Are you? Eh? Eh? Eh? Tell me.'

'No, no,' I cried. 'Not me.'

He kept on for long enough, but that was the worst of it over. He made another prayer before he was done, but it was a quiet prayer for him, no great noise about it at all. Despite the pleading of my mother, he would not take a bite nor even a drink of tea. I was not sorry to see him go, I am telling you.

Tomas Caogach came back in from walking him to the road. 'Well, well,' he said, rubbing his hands, that pleased with himself you would have thought he had been up at the Games and seen great feats on the field, 'whoever heard the like o' the *Ceistear* at the making of a prayer? There is not a minister his equal.'

'And him not for taking a cup o' tea, far less a bite,' my mother said. 'It is a wonder to me how he keeps on the go, he is that hard on himself, poor man.'

She gathered up her pails, and made off to the byre, well enough pleased with herself, for all her weeping. Tomas Caogach sat down at the table, and got out his pipe and tobacco tin. He had not taken a smoke after supper for fear the smell would linger, but he was not going to miss his third pipe of the day now that the *Ceistear* had gone. I shut my eyes, and kept them shut, even when I heard him get up and make for the door. 'You do well to sit quiet, boy,' he said, as he went by. 'Think on the words o' the *Ceistear*, and heed them well from this day on.'

I counted up to a hundred, saying to myself over and over again, *Do not look right off, and it will be there. Do not look right off, and it will be there.*

I opened my eyes. The tobacco tin lay on the table. I was across the floor in the blink of an eye, and had the tin open and the coil of thick black twist in my hand. My eyes had not been deceiving me; there was tobacco there to last Tomas Caogach a twelvemonth and more. Mr Ferguson must set a high price on poachers to hand out presents like that. I looked around for a knife, and heard a sound at my back. Before I could move, a big bony hand had clamped around my wrist.

'Stealing now, is it?' Tomas Caogach cried, near beside himself with rage, 'and the *Ceistear* not minutes away from the house.'

As he raised his free hand to strike me, I twisted out of his grip, and ran behind the fire. The fire was set in the centre of the floor; the flaming peats, and the big iron cooking pot on its blackened chain, made a barrier between us. He edged around the fire, crouched low, like a wrestler, making ready to rush me. I backed slowly away, eyes on his face, gleaming red in the peat fire flames. There was no sound, save the harsh rasping of his breath, and the loud thumping of my heart.

I made a dart to my left, and he turned clumsily to block me. The path to the door was open. I changed direction, and was off out the door, running as I had never run before, the coil of tobacco clutched tight in my fist.

7

Only the broken skeleton of the old wreck remained; the splintered stump of her stem curving down to join the heavy keel, long settled in the sand: that, and a few bare ribs of her frame, was all that was left to show what she had once been. She lay well clear of the tideline on the shore below the inn, where she had been swept years ago by a big spring tide that had a sou'-westerly gale at its back. It was a good place for keeping an eye on the Lodge, and far enough away from Tomas Caogach for safety, right across the water from our township, at the other end of the horse-shoe bay.

Sitting on the shore beside the old wreck, the coil of tobacco in my pocket a constant reminder of the wrath of Tomas Caogach, my mind was in a turmoil. I was thinking of his face, fierce in the peat fire flames, as he crouched ready to spring; of the great bank of thick white fog creeping in from the sea, wondering how long it would take to blanket the bay, drift inland, and shut the light from the sky; of what like it would be aboard the beauty of a yacht that lay at anchor out from the Lodge, slowly swinging on the tide; of Marsali — was she still on the go in the kitchen, or waiting in her room for the lamps to be doused, and the house to sleep? — and it came to me that something was wrong.

It is a queer thing, the mind. Many's the time I have wondered what guides a salmon through the deeps to its chosen river, but the force that drives the salmon is not more strange than the way your mind can be teeming with thoughts — an impatient flock of them jostling for attention, more than enough for one frail mind to tackle — and, unbeknown to you, is busy at other things altogether, digging deep at them on the quiet, and not letting on to you, until it has got everything sorted.

It was the wreck that was wrong. Part of the after end of the keel, and its bolted ribs, was missing. The last foot or so of the barnacle-crusted and pitted keel had been dug out of the sand; there was an empty trough beyond where the rest had lain. And the keel ended, neat and new, in a fresh saw-cut. The sawn end of the blackened keel had a light brown eye at the centre that Stockholm tar and age and weather had not been able to reach. I got down on my hands and knees, feeling the ridging in the old oak where the saw teeth had ripped through the wood.

Someone had made off with the after end of the skeleton of the old wreck. When the factor got word, there would be more than Mata the tinker in trouble, and not just because we were forbidden to lift drift timber and the like from the shore. The old wreck was special. One of the gentry who came to the Lodge was a great painter, and they said that a painting he had made of the wreck had been bought by the Queen herself. For sure, all the English visitors to the inn always came down the hill to the shore, and made for that blackened skeleton of a boat as if there was something magic in the remains.

A girl's voice, right at my back, said, 'Can I help?'

An English voice, loud and quick. I was that startled, I remained where I was, crouched on my hands and knees. Out of the corner of my eye, I saw the soft leather of her boots, a dusting of fine sand across the dainty toes. I got to my feet, and faced her.

She might have been half an inch taller than me, but she was no older, that was a sure thing. She was dressed in a dark skirt and a white blouse, with a shining silver belt enclosing her waist, her long fair hair held back with a black ribbon. She said again, in that quick English voice, 'Can I help?'

'Help?' I said, wondering what on earth she was on about.

'Help you look.'

'Look?'

'Do you understand English?' she said, speaking that slow and deliberate you would have thought I was a bairn, not old enough to have seen the inside of a school.

'Aye, fine,' I said, feeling the blood rushing to my face, 'I understand English.'

We stood there, eyeing each other, and although my face was flaming, she did not seem so sure of herself now. 'Haven't you lost something?' she said.

'Lost something?' I said, the words out before I realised that I was at it again, turning her words back on her, and making them sound as if I had no notion of their true meaning. She must think I was lacking. I looked down at my feet, stained with dirt, itching something terrible where sand had lodged between my toes. I rubbed one foot against the other to take out the itch, and was suddenly conscious of the richness of the soft leather of her boots. She had never gone barefoot in her life, I would take an oath on that. She gave a nervous sort of a laugh, and I looked up, thinking my ears had deceived me. But no, she was not laughing at me. 'I'm sorry,' she said. 'I made a mistake. I thought you had lost something, and were looking for it.'

'No, I was just looking,' I said, the words coming awkward to my tongue, and not just because it was English words I was seeking. 'At the old wreck,' I added.

'Do you live here?'

I nodded.

'Whereabouts?'

I pointed across the bay to our township. The bank of sea fog was creeping steady around the headland of Ru Idrigil. Once it rounded the point, the thick white bank would soon roll in and swallow the bay; that was always the way of it with a summer fog coming in off the sea.

'You are lucky,' she said.

'Lucky?'

'Living in such a beautiful place.'

'Beautiful?' I could not stop repeating words after her, like a bairn learning a lesson. I was wild at myself.

'It looks lovely,' she said, her blue eyes fairly sparkling with delight, 'the land all green down to the bay, and tucked in so cosy with the hill behind. And all those tiny houses with the thatched roofs; they look as if they had just grown out of the ground all by themselves — like . . . like mushrooms. And — look! — each little house has its own plume of smoke, like a blue banner. It's . . . it's beautiful.'

What would you expect from a fire but smoke, and it to rise slow in the still air of a summer's night? I very near put the thought into words, only held back by the knowledge that she was a stranger who knew no better, but I could not stop myself saying, 'There is many a one cursed the day they were put there,' suddenly wild at the nerve of her telling me I was lucky to be living on the shore in that certain-sure English voice of hers, and herself ignorant of the condition of the people; staying at the inn, I would not wonder, waited on hand and foot — or one of a party off the big white yacht in the bay, a big cabin all to herself, with carpets on the floor, and water out of a tap, and servants galore on board, eager to jump to her bidding. I knew about the yachts, and the gear they carried. Marsali had told me often enough.

'Put there?' she said, frowning. 'What do you mean?'

I toed a circle in the sand, not wanting to argue with a stranger. 'Removed from their own good crofts,' I said, 'and put down to the shore.'

I believe I would have held my tongue after that, if she had not trumpeted, 'What rot!' She pointed across the bay to our township, as if I was the stranger and she the knowing guide, adding, 'I daresay people have lived there for hundreds and hundreds of years.'

'That is where you are wrong,' I burst out. 'See you,' — I turned a quivering finger to the cleft in the hill, thick with trees on the lower slopes, where the Conon flowed through the glen on its way to the sea — 'up the glen yonder, that is where they lived for hundreds and hundreds of years, where there was great grazing for their cattle, and good land for to work their crops. What folk would live on the edge o' the sea, with only a scrap o' poor land for corn and potatoes, and naught but a stretch o' black moor to graze their beasts, if they were not forced?'

'Forced?' she said, frowning again. 'Surely not.'

'And my own father with the thatch torn from his roof?' I said hotly. 'Was that not forced?'

'When did this happen?' she said.

'A long time ago.'

'It didn't sound a long time ago, listening to you.'

'Neither it was, not all that long ago.'

'How long?'

'The year I was born.'

'Well?'

'Fourteen — getting on for fifteen years ago.'

'By whom?'

'How do you mean?'

She pointed across the bay again. 'You said they were "put there" — by force.'

'So they were.'

'But who did it? Who forced them there?'

She was as bad as the *Ceistear* with the questions, but there was a difference. Her wide blue eyes looked straight into mine, and there was no guile in them, I would swear to that. 'The Sheriff Officer came with papers,' I said. 'It was the law just.'

'To tear the thatch from your father's roof?'

I shrugged. 'If the Sheriff Officer has got the right papers, you must go, that is all there is about it.'

'But why?' she said. 'I don't understand.'

'Why they were cleared from the glen?'

'Yes.'

'To make room for one man,' I said. 'Himself and his sheep. Wi' hundreds o' sheep and just the — .'

A voice called, 'Coo-eee!'

I saw her first, a stout woman in black, standing on the shore by the path to the smithy and the mill. She was waving as if her life depended upon it, not pleased at all by the look of her. The girl waved back, and called, 'Coming.' She turned to me, and said, 'I must go. Isn't it time you were going home? Whatever will your father say?'

'My father is dead,' I said.

'I'm sorry.' She put a hand on my arm. 'What's your name?'

'Calum Og.'

She nodded, and turned away. I plucked up my courage, and said boldly to her back, 'What is your name?'

She stopped, and swung round, looking at me as if it was she who had asked a question. The stout woman called again. The girl flipped a hand at her without turning round. I was wondering if she had heard me right when she gave a quick smile, and said, 'Elizabeth.' She ran, skipping, to the stout woman in black. I watched the two of them until they were past the smithy and lost in the trees.

There was a chill in the air now that the sea fog was filling the bay. It had swallowed the yacht and the most of our township. The Lodge, standing in the very centre of the horse-shoe bay, would be the last to go. There were lights showing at the front windows. I hoped the lamps would be out before the fog closed in; I had no fancy to be wandering through the grounds not knowing if the factor was safely tethered in bed or still on the go. Sitting with my back against the stem of the old wreck, I settled down to wait, thinking not of Tomas Caogach, for a wonder, or even Marsali, but the girl called Elizabeth who thought our township was beautiful.

'What kept you, boy?' Marsali demanded, her voice shrill, putting me in mind of our mother, she was that complaining. She pulled me into the woodshed, and closed the door. 'I thought you were never coming.'

'I was afraid to chance it,' I said, 'for fear the factor was still up. With the fog that thick, I had no way of knowing whether the lamps were out or not.'

'If we are not smart about it the house will be on the stir for a new day,' she said, but the sharpness had gone from her voice, anger abated now that I was along with her.

51

Marsali had come prepared. She lit the stump of a candle, perched on the big chopping block, and unwrapped a linen cloth. I watched her select a beauty of a piece for me — white baker's bread, and between the bread a slice of ham thick enough to sole your boots, and stand a winter's wear no bother. She took one herself, and sank her teeth into it. She had the strongest, whitest teeth I had ever seen on a girl, Marsali.

'What a day I have had,' she mumbled, her mouth full of bread and ham, 'scrubbing, cleaning, polishing — as if we had not given every speck o' dust a fright the day the factor went off, without starting away again this morning cleaning the house from top to bottom. Supposing the Queen herself had been coming to stay, I doubt there would have been such a to-do. And all for Lady Maxwell-Drummond, and herself not — .'

'Marsali,' I butted in, 'if you knew who they had at me today you would — .'

'But imagine all that cleaning,' she protested, not prepared to let me get a word in now that she had emptied her mouth, 'and herself off again first thing in the morning.'

'Who?'

Marsali gave an impatient snort. 'Lady Maxwell-Drummond. That big yacht in the bay — English gentry, friends o' the laird. She is away with them first thing in the morning for a cruise. She will be gone for a week they say. And all that polishing for a — .'

'*Ist* with your polishing,' I said. 'Wait you, until you hear what I have to tell. We were off to the peat bog first thing, and you know what like Tomas Caogach is but you have no idea the way he was going at the lifting. He was fairly killing himself — and me and the *cailleach* along with him — and just because we could not get them all on their feet he — .'

'Why not?' Marsali said, taking another bite at her piece. 'If you were at it all day you should have got the bog lifted no bother.'

'We had to make back to the house early. He had a visitor coming special to see me. You know what? He had the *Ceistear* at me, special.You can laugh, Marsali. Questions! You never heard the like. And the time he was making a prayer! On and on and on. My knees were cracking before he was done. And the great roars the man lets out, and him so wee. Our mother was weeping.'

'She would enjoy it fine,' Marsali said. 'That woman is never happy unless she is weeping.'

'This is great ham,' I said, stuffing the remains of the piece into my mouth. 'How do you suppose our father ever came to marry her?'

'Who knows?'

'It is a wonder to me.'

'Maybe she was different when she was young.'

'More like you?'

'No, not like me,' Marsali said. 'You will never see me put upon by the like of Tomas Caogach. Wait you, boy, the day will come when I am clear o' this place, and go my own way.'

She would too. She may have had our mother's colouring, but there was a lot of our father in Marsali.

She gave me the biggest of the two ham pieces left on the cloth, taking the smaller one herself. 'They say they have never seen the factor so wild,' she said. 'He has had all the keepers hauled to the house — the ground officer as well. Pity your tinker, Calum Og. Lady Elizabeth and her governess went off for a walk, and they were no sooner gone from the house than I could hear the factor roaring at the keepers — and me in the kitchen wi' the door shut.'

'What is a governess?'

'A kind of a teacher. The gentry are not for sending their children to the school along wi' the — .'

'That would ha' suited me fine. A pity we were not gentry, Marsali.'

'Be quiet, you clown. You were clear o' the school when you were eleven. Amn't I after telling you the gentry take the teachers home with them, only they call them a fancy name. A governess is a teacher just. Lady Elizabeth is your age, and she has — .'

'Lady Who?'

'If it is not your ears needing cleaning, you are slow, boy. You had not started in on your piece when I was telling of the day we have had turning the place upside down, and all for that Lady Elizabeth Maxwell-Drummond, and herself not my age. I never knew a girl so young could be a right Lady. That is what I am telling you, if only you would listen. The girl has a teacher with her, only the teacher is called a governess, so you need not be thinking the gentry have a great time of it staying clear of the school.'

'Lady Elizabeth?' I said, choking on the ham piece. I put the rest of it back on the cloth, my appetite gone.

'Aye, the laird's cousin. All that fuss for a lassie no older than yourself. What is the matter?' she said. 'You must be ailing, Calum Og, if you cannot finish a piece.'

'I had plenty,' I said. 'It was great, Marsali.'

'It would take more than the *Ceistear* to put me off my food,' she said, picking up what was left of my piece, and finishing it off. She licked her fingers clean. 'Well, if you are for having a word wi' your tinker, we had best make haste.'

She got to her feet, and snuffed the candle. It was easy done; a thumb and finger coming together and the flame was gone. If only words could be snuffed that easy, I thought, as I followed her out into the night.

He must have had his ears pricked, fine honed for the least sound, awaiting my coming. When I called softly, he answered at once, and there was a something in his voice that had not been there before. I guessed straight off the reason why he sounded so down in the mouth. 'Has the factor been at you, Mata?' I said, feeling the big coil of tobacco in my pocket, thinking to myself he would cheer up if he knew what he had coming to him.

'No, not himself,' he said, 'the long fellow — the Head Keeper — and two others. They put a rod on me.'

'A what?'

'A measuring rod.'

'You mean, they measured you?'

'Aye, they were after measuring me. I am fear'd, Calum Og.'

'Fear'd, Mata?'

'O' the measuring.'

'Why?'

'I have heard them say it is always done that way before a hanging.'

'A hanging?'

'Aye, they are after measuring the one that is for the hanging. It has to do wi' the rope, and the drop they give him.'

'Away!'

'Right enough, Calum Og, I have heard them tell of it, them that know.'

'Maybe so, Mata, but not you. They cannot hang you for lifting a salmon.'

'Not one salmon — five, boy. And many a score besides. Hundreds just. They know that fine.'

'Supposing it was thousands, Mata, they cannot hang you. There has got to be a court and the law and the like for a hanging.'

'In this place? There is only the one law in this place, and that is the law o' the factor.'

'Still an' all, he cannot do a hanging, not even the factor. He would have to get the right law in on it for a hanging.' There was something else — what was it? — I needed it bad to lift the worry from him. 'And a judge,' I crowed, triumphant.

'*Ist!*' Marsali hissed.

'There has got to be a judge,' I said, lowering my voice. 'There was never a hanging without a judge, and the factor would need to go the length of Inverness for to find one.'

'Is that right?' he asked.

'As I am here.'

'Are you sure, Calum Og?'

'Certain sure.'

'Well, well, they put a scare in me,' he said, more cheerful now, 'what wi' that measuring an' all, and the Keeper and his men not saying a word.'

Marsali was hissing at me to go. One of the dogs was growling, deep in his throat, ready to bark by the sound of it. I strained on tiptoe, reaching up and feeling for the narrow opening in the wall above the door. 'I have got tobacco, Mata,' I said quickly. 'I will toss it through the slit above the door. Right?'

'Good on you, boy,' he said.

I flipped the coil through the slit, and waited, calling softly to Marsali that I was coming. Whatever Tomas Caogach's worries, hanging or the jail was not numbered among them. Mata's need was the greatest.

'*Dhia!*' he said, wonder in his voice, 'What a weight o' tobacco, Calum Og. How did you manage it, boy?'

Marsali seized my arm before I could reply, and pulled me away, talking sharp to the dogs to quieten them. She hurried me past the kennels, and along the path through the bushes. If I had known that those words of Mata's were to be the last I would ever hear from him in this world I would have shaken off Marsali's grip, and gone back to the old meal store. But that is always the way of it. We never take time to say all that needs to be said, and there is always a something tugging at our arm that has to be heeded first.

From the moment I parted from Marsali, until I stood at the door of the house, it was not the thought of having to face Tomas Caogach that had me quaking, but fear of what the laird's cousin, Lady Elizabeth Maxwell-Drummond, might do. And if you think I was a right clown to speak so free to a stranger, let me tell you it would take a wise man to know that such a slip of a girl could have a title to her name, and be a cousin of the laird. I had always thought of the laird as a man well up in years, and all his relations the same — and I still could not make out how a girl so young could have a proper title.

Supposing she told the factor what had passed between us? That was Tomas Caogach, and the rest of us, cleared from his croft before another day dawned, nothing surer. Mata was right enough saying that the only law in the place was the law of the factor, and I had been fool enough to question the law-maker; to say that we had been cleared to the shore so that his brother could put the whole of Glenuig under sheep, and get the good of it for himself. But there was more to it than that. It was the laird I was getting at. The factor was no more than the servant of the laird, so he must have been carrying out his master's orders. And the girl was the laird's own cousin! My mother always made out my tongue would hang me.

But Marsali had said the girl was away for a cruise in the big yacht first thing in the morning. Maybe the stout woman in black — her governess; and the same one looking a right warrior — had rushed her away to bed, and she had no chance of a word with the factor. Maybe he would be out in the morning — he often took a ride first thing — and she would board the yacht without speaking to him. And supposing the weather turned bad, a gale got up — there were often bad gales in the month of July — and the yacht was stormbound for days. Maybe she would take such a scunner to the place she would order the laird's friends to make straight for Strome — being a Lady she would have the right to give orders, young and all as she was — and take the new Skye Railway to Inverness, and make back from whatever she had come without showing her face near the Lodge again. But what if she made straight for the laird, and told him? Maybe the laird was away in Africa, though, and by the time he came home again she would have forgotten every word about me, forgotten all the things I had said about folk cursing the day they were cleared to the shore, forgotten that the two of us had ever stood by the skeleton of the old wreck, as the fogbank rolled in from the sea.

Or what if she had already told on me to the factor, and that hot-tempered man had sent word to Tomas Caogach that he was to be gone from the place. If that was the way of it, he would have more to worry about than his missing tobacco, and so would I.

The door was shut, but he was waiting up for me, Tomas Caogach; I knew that when I saw the glow of the lamp lightening the dark eye of the window. A corncrake down the croft was croaking away good style. I listened to him for long enough, as if he had a message for my ears alone, before I managed to force my hand to take a hold of the latch. I opened the door, and shut it quick at my back, in case fear got the better of me.

The two of them were waiting up for me, sitting side by side on the bench, the open Bible between them. My mother was weeping, the tears flowing free. Fresh peats were blazing on the fire. I crossed the floor, and stood with my back to the flames, facing the pair of them.

Tomas Caogach looked at me. He made no move to rise and seize me and strike me down. He just sat there on the bench, his good left eye anchored fast on my face, as if he could not believe that it was me standing before him. The *cailleach* never raised her head, and her sobbing never ceased. Seeing the two of them looking that stricken, I was certain sure that the laird's cousin had told on me, and the factor had sent word that they must go. It was as well that I held my tongue.

Tomas Caogach held out his hand. 'The tobacco,' he said.

'It is gone,' I said, my voice sounding strangely loud in my ears.

'Gone?' He tasted the word on his tongue, and his mouth twisted, as if he had taken gall. 'Gone?' he said. 'Where?'

I looked down at my feet, not saying a word.

He was across the floor in one swift bound, and had me by the shoulder. He shook me until my teeth rattled. 'Where is my tobacco?' he said, through clenched teeth. 'Where? What have you done wi' my tobacco, thief that you are?'

I kept my mouth shut.

My mother looked up, her red eyes streaming. 'Better he had perished an innocent bairn, like many another in the place,' she said, 'than it should come to this.'

Tomas Caogach tightened his grip on my shoulder. It felt as if the bone must crack. 'Spite, is it?' he cried. 'Wicked spite just, throwing away my good tobacco that I had in a present.' He was near weeping. I never thought to see Tomas Caogach near weeping.

'Away to your bed, Iseabal,' he said. 'It is myself will sort this one.' And to me, as she got up obediently to go, 'Off wi' your jersey and shirt, boy. There is only one way to get the truth out of the like o' you.'

He let go of my shoulder, and strode across to the bench. He closed the open Bible, and laid it on the table. As I pulled off my jersey, I saw him seize his hazel switch. He bent it near double in his big fists, and let it spring open again.

8

I had my shirt in my hands when I knelt at the bench, holding it bunched on the wooden seat, pillowing my forehead. The first cut of the switch, the full strength of his arm behind it, seared my flesh as if a branding iron had been lifted straight from the fire and clapped across my back. My head could not have jerked up any faster supposing the shirt had suddenly burst into flames. I made a grab for the bench, got my hands around the back of the seat, and hung on for dear life. Dipping my head down, I took a bite on a mouthful of shirt, the way a starving man, if his arms were bound, would use his jaws to snatch at food set before him.

I did not think any hurt could be as bad as the terrible sharp bite of that first cut — until the second one came. He took his time before he brought the switch down again, so that I shrank from the blow a score of times before it fell; and it bit all the deeper for that, making me groan on the gag that I had clamped between my teeth.

Three, four, five, six, seven. All quick, one after the other, hot knives slicing the flesh, a spreading fire burning my back. I was choking on the gag, but I forced my face deeper into the cloth, praying he would not hear the noises that came from me.

Eight, nine, ten. My back aflame, scorching, searing; the terrible heat of it making me sweat as I had never sweated before — face, neck, chest, belly, thighs; the sweat running free. The shirt was soaking wet under my face.

I heard his voice. Not the soft, quiet drone Marsali was so good at mocking, but the hoarse, breathless voice of a stranger. 'What have you done wi' my tobacco?'

Silence. Only a faint moaning, far-off in the distance. Was that me? Or noises in my head? Or a stir of wind outside the house? I could hear lungs greedy for air, panting like a bellows going, drawing harsh, rasping breaths. Mine or his? Not mine, surely, my face buried in the shirt, teeth tight clenched on the cloth.

The beating started again, scourging my back, no break between, the strokes lashing down one after the other. Not a hazel switch, thin and light, no weight to it at all, not his thin switch of hazel, surely. This was heavy iron, rough and jagged, not smooth at all, great spiked teeth clawing, digging, tearing deep into my back, fierce as the teeth on the tacksman's big harrow.

The voice of the stranger again. '*What have you done wi' my tobacco?*'

The *Ceistear* was always telling us boys stories of the martyrs in olden days, how they suffered terrible tortures for their faith. I went to Seumas the shoemaker with the *Ceister's* stories about the martyrs, and asked him how it was that men in olden times were able to endure such tortures for their faith, thinking — although I never let on — that had it been me I would have cried out to the torturers to stop, no matter what. Seumas told me that the body would not let a man bear more than he was able, that when the pain became too bad you would lose your senses, and know no more.

Seumas the shoemaker lied to me, or else he did not know and was making up stories of his own. I know that now, and I will tell you for why. If old Seumas had told me true, I could not have heard that voice — the voice of a stranger, hoarse and breathless — saying the same words again and again and again.

'*What have you done wi' my tobacco?*'

'*What have you done wi' my tobacco?*'

'*What have you done wi' my tobacco?*'

I heard that voice, and felt the switch biting into my back, and me drowning in a sea of pain — a long drowning that was never done — always knowing he was standing above me, always hearing his panting breath, and that voice always asking the same question, and always, always feeling the sharp teeth of the switch.

I do not know how long it lasted — it could have been hours or days or weeks; the only count of time that had any meaning to me was the count of the cuts of the switch, and I had lost track of them long since — all awareness shrivelled into a white-hot flame of pain that was melting my bones, eating away my being, diminishing me entire, as I knelt at the bench, hands clawing at the wood as if they would never leave hold.

There came an end to it, an end to the stranger's voice asking, always asking; only the pain went on, burning so deep that the drawing of a breath raked it red raw, the way a smouldering fire quickens into flame at the puff of a bellows.

I stood up. I was like a cripple trying to straighten himself from the prison of his twisted limbs after a lifetime bent double. I stood upright, swaying on my feet, the shirt trailing down my front, still clamped tight between my teeth. I got my jaws open, and let the sweat-soaked shirt fall to the floor Learning to walk again, I turned away from the bench, like one picking his way barefoot through a multitude of sharp flints.

Tomas Caogach stood before me, the switch clenched in his fists. He had it bent across his chest, and he was weeping — weeping, Tomas Caogach! As I stared at him, he half turned, and cast the switch into the fire. I took a slow step forward, no thought in my head but how to reach the bed, and he backed away from me; backed away, step by step, like a man afraid, as I moved forward. When he came up against my bed in the wall, and could retreat no further, he gave a cry — half groan, half wail — and ducked his head and ran out of the kitchen to his own room. I reached the box-bed, and held on to the wooden frame until I could summon the strength to climb in. I fell into bed, flat on my face, my back on fire.

My thighs felt wet. The shame of it eased the pain, if you can believe such a thing. I put a hand down to my leg, and gazed stupidly at the stain on my palm. I had not wet myself; it was blood on my hand. My back must be cut and bleeding, the blood trickling down my legs. I lay still, breathing hard, the harsh croak of the corncrake down the croft loud in my ears. The bird kept on and on and on, near as bad as Tomas Caogach's snores, and himself silent for a wonder.

I awoke with my mother bending over me, the lamp in her hand. She was not weeping, but her face in the guttering flame of the *cruisgean* was as near weeping as it would ever be without the tears flowing. She never said a word, but went to the fire and blew it into life, and brought fresh peats, and heated water, and bathed my back with a soft cloth. Her hands were that gentle you would have thought it was a baby she was tending, but the least touch was like a nailed boot treading heavy on my flesh.

'Why must you vex him so, boy?' she said, when she was done. 'Why?'

'Why must he do the like o' this to me?'

'The tobacco — ,' she started.

'I paid for the tobacco,' I said, 'paid dear.'

'Hush, boy, it is done,' she said. 'There will be no more of it.'

'He will never take a stick to me again,' I said, thinking of the look on his face as he backed away from me and fled the room, wondering how it had come to pass that Tomas Caogach had been broken without a blow being struck by me.

The *cailleach* never spoke, but she was still standing by my bed, her thin grey hair loose on her shoulders, when I went back to sleep.

She woke me in the morning with a bowl of tea, not sparing with the makings for once, the tea good and strong the way I like it. I slept again; a heavy, dreamless sleep. It was afternoon when I awoke, the sun well past the meridian, slanting in at the open door, cutting a bright swathe across the earthen floor and dimming the peat fire flames. The *cailleach* was sitting close by my bed on the birch-bough stool.

'Where is he?' I asked.

'Away at the peats,' she said, as if she had every right to be taking her ease on the stool.

It was changed days, Tomas Caogach away at the bog lifting peats, and my mother sitting idle at home, and me in bed, but you would not have known from the way she spoke. She got up from the stool and made brose, and it was clear that I was the one to be waited on, not Tomas Caogách. She even wanted to spoon the brose to me, as if I was a bairn again, but I was not having that. It is awkward, right enough, eating in bed, lying on your belly, but I propped myself up on one elbow, and managed well enough.

I was still in bed, dozing on and off, no sooner awake than I was sliding back into sleep again, when Gilleasbuig, the ground officer, came to the door. Once I had heard his voice, and taken in what he had to say, that was me done with sleep. It was a harsh awakening to come from a voice as smooth as treacle.

Supposing God had given the factor the makings of a ground officer, and shown him how to put such a creature together with his own hands, he could not have fashioned one better suited to the job than Gilleasbuig. Gilleasbuig was the eyes and ears of the factor in the place, and he carried the marks of his trade plain for all to see — quick, darting eyes, fit to spot a new leather lace in the broken boot of a man claiming to be without money for the rent; his big ears, sticking out from his head like sails, always on the flap for news he could carry back to his master. He was great at whispered confidences, hoping his own story would draw forth a better; always ready with the right word to nudge along those whose tongues were too guarded, murmuring, 'Surely not,' or 'I doubt you have got it wrong,' or 'I can hardly believe the like o' that,' — fly to use disbelief as a goad to prick from the cautious more than they had thought to tell.

If we had grievances, we were supposed to make them known to Gilleasbuig, and he had the authority to take our grievances to the factor. But there were none so bold as to complain, and risk being branded a trouble-maker in the eyes of the factor. That is the worst of it when a factor has no Gaelic. The tongue of the people is in another man's mouth, and what way can they know what he is telling the factor about them.

Gilleasbuig called a greeting from the door, not the usual purr in his voice, but oily enough for all that. 'No, I am not for taking a seat, Mistress,' he said, the words issuing slow and smooth, 'the dogcart is waiting for me at the road. I have many a call to make yet, and the afternoon near spent. When the factor says word must be got round smart, there can be no dallying for the likes o' me, I am the one that must jump to it, it is myself knows that, and me on the go since first thing.' He drew breath, and mopped his sweating face with a white handkerchief near as big as a table-cloth, his pale blue eyes making a quick survey of the room. 'Every man in the place is to be at the smithy tonight, once the sun is down. Every man, mind. The factor is to be speaking.'

'The factor? — speaking at the smithy?' my mother said, that amazed you would have thought she had been told the *Ceistear* had been carried home drunk after dancing an eightsome reel in the taproom of the inn.

Gilleasbuig was scurrying away before the words were out of her mouth, and that was not like him. 'Aye, the smithy,' he called over his shoulder. 'Once the sun is down. The factor is to say what is to be done wi' the tinker they caught poaching.'

I had my feet on the floor before the *cailleach* got back from the door, and there was some row — well, not so much a row as her pleading with me to get back to bed. She kept on at me for long enough, but I believe she knew I was not to be moved, and she gave in when I agreed to let her put ointment on my back.

'It is great stuff,' she said, 'I had it from the packman the last time he was round. Moonseed Bitters it is called, made special for the gentry, the packman says, at a place in England. It will take the soreness out o' your back, you see.'

She scooped ointment from the pot into the palm of her hand, and I bent my back while she smoothed the stuff on with her fingertips. It was so cold it burned me, but that was nothing to the tips of her fingers digging into my back like harrows. I gritted my teeth to stop from crying out, thankful she could not see my face.

63

'There,' she said, when she was done, fine pleased with herself, 'the Moonseed Bitters will put you right, boy, never fear.'

'Aye, fine,' I said, wondering how I was going to get the shirt on my back. In truth, it was not easy with herself looking on, watching my every move, and me having to pretend that I was not feeling a thing, when every touch of the shirt against my back meant a raking by wicked barbs, every single one of them a separate agony.

'You are sweating, boy,' she said.

I walked stiffly to the door, so that she could not see my face. 'Aye, it is close,' I said.

So it was. The air was still, that heavy with heat it seemed to be pressing down on you, all the weight of the circling hill at its back. The sun was very near as dim as a clouded moon, it was that thickly veiled in haze. The light seemed to be draining fast from the sky, turning the loch black. There was not the least ripple on the water; it was a dead calm, the water flat as oil. A heron rose from the shore at the foot of our croft, and flew off with a lazy beat of wing.

'There is going to be a thunderplump,' my mother said. 'I can feel it in the air. Ach, well, your uncle should have the rest of the peats lifted before the rain comes.'

It was the first time she had spoken of him all day, and I was not so slow that I could not see she was trying to make the peace, wanting to show that this was the same as any other day — himself at the peats as he had been the day before — and what had happened last night was past, and best forgotten. But that was not the way of it at all.

I sat down on the bench to wait for Tomas Caogach. It would be too easy to make off before he showed face. I was not for letting him forget that he had backed away from me, and the day of his dominion was done.

9

He did not look at me when he came in. All the *cailleach* got from him when she told him of the factor's message was a grunt. It was the same when we took our supper, not a word out of him, excepting the prayer before and after, and he was up from the table as soon as he had sounded '*Amen*' — off to change into his good Sabbath suit and stiff white collar, seeing he was away to a meeting, and the factor speaking.

He came back into the kitchen in his stocking soles, carrying his best boots. He sat down on the stool to put them on, leaving the bench free to me and the *cailleach*. He had not forgotten last night, that was easy seen, or he would never have humbled himself on the low stool. I got up, and made for the door.

'Where are you away to, boy?' he said.

'The meeting,' I said, standing still at the open door, but not bothering to look back at him.

He gave a grunt. I glanced over my shoulder as I went out the door. He had his head down, lacing his boots.

'Don't be staying up half the night at the shoemaker's,' my mother called after me.

There was no ready echo from Tomas Caogach, the way there had always been in the old days. Tomas Caogach was silent.

The great sea of people parted to admit the factor and his men. The multitude moved as one, without a word being spoken, splitting down the middle and opening a clear lane to the smithy. Looking down at them from my perch astride a bough of the old ash, it put me in mind of the story in the Book about the sea dividing to give passage to Moses and the children of Israel. But it was not a Moses I was seeing, pursued by Pharaoh and his chariots; it was the factor and his servants, bringing his prisoner to judgement.

The factor came first, on his high-stepping black stallion, the beast not pleased at being reined to a slow walk, followed by Mr Ferguson and Gilleasbuig, and behind them Mata the tinker, surrounded by four keepers. As the procession passed through the crowd to the open double doors of the smithy, the people surged together again, the boys at the back straining to get a sight of what was going on.

The factor turned the black stallion, and halted him facing the crowd. Mr Ferguson took up a stance on his right, Gilleasbuig on his left. Mata was brought to a stop beyond Gilleasbuig, close guarded by the keepers, two on either side of him. He was dwarfed by his guards; a little, ragged, barefoot man, head down, black hair fringing his eyes, his head not level with the shoulders of the smallest of the four. His right cheek was swollen. It was a while before it came to me that he must have a big wad of tobacco pouched there, ready for a chew when there were no eyes on him. The thought soothed my back better than the Moonseed Bitters.

There was a hush, as if everyone present had drawn a deep breath and held it locked in their lungs; a quiet so deep there was dread in it, setting the heart beating faster. It was a dread fashioned, I believe, by the night itself every bit as much as the presence of the factor and his men, and the sight of Tormod Gobha, the smith — as easy-natured a man as you could wish to meet, his broad moon of a face forever beaming — unsmiling, arms folded across his leather apron, solemn as an executioner. It was the darkest midsummer night at sundown that I had ever seen; the sky a lowering black, no afterglow in the west to lighten the gloom. There was not a tremor in the leaves of the aspen at the back of the smithy, the air fairly steaming in the close, still heat. The only sound was the snorting of the stallion, and the jingling of his harness as he tossed his head, until the loud English voice of the factor barked its message.

He pointed a gloved hand at Mata. 'This tinker is a salmon poacher. I have no doubt he is known to many of you. If I handed him over to the police, he would go to prison. In prison, he would be better housed, better clothed and better fed than he has ever been at any time in his miserable life. Prison would not deter him, so I shall deal with him in my own way. It was quick and easy for him to enter the estate: I propose to make it slow and difficult for him to leave. The rest of his clan have fled. He will seek to join them. It will be a journey he will not want to risk repeating. That is why I have summoned you from every township on the estate. When I set this man free, he is not to be given food or water or any assistance of any kind. You are expressly forbidden to relieve him of his burden. Any one of you — or your womenfolk or children — disobeying my orders will suffer instant eviction. That is all.'

The most of them there were not understanding a word of it, having only the Gaelic. Even those who thought they were well versed in English were only catching the odd word or two, seeing the speed he rattled it out in that queer, clipped accent of his. That was where Gilleasbuig came in. It was the ground officer's job to put the factor's words into the Gaelic, so that none of us had the excuse that we did not understand what he was saying.

'The most o' you are well acquaint wi' the tinker here,' Gilleasbuig bawled, making a fair imitation of the *Ceistear* the way his voice boomed out at the silent crowd. 'The factor is not for putting him to the jail — the jail would be a holiday for him just. But he has to be sorted, the same one, if the gentry are to get the good o' their fishings — fishings they have laid out big money on.

'You and me, we know the likes o' this fellow. Him and his kind are not easy sorted. The first chance he got he would make back to the river and think nothing of it. Unless he was learned a lesson; learned it the hard way; learned it deep in the muscles of his back.

'Think on, have any o' you ever laid eyes on a tinker carting a heavy load, eh? You and me, we are bent low often enough trailing home creels o' seaware and peats on our back, but not the tinker. The tinker steps light and easy, the way this fellow did down to the river. Well, the factor is not for making it easy for him when he foots it out for to find his tribe, and them away the other side o' the island. He will have a load on his back, and that load is to stay on his back. Before he is clear o' the estate boundaries he will be desperate for a drink and a bite. He is to stay desperate. That is the factor's solemn orders. Any tenant o' the estate giving a hand to the tinker, that is him finished — cleared from the place on the instant. That is the word o' the factor.'

Turning to the factor, Gilleasbuig said, in English, 'I told them, sir.'

'You are sure you made my orders clear?' the factor asked.

'Word for word, sir,' the ground officer said.

'Very well. Get the smith to work.'

Gilleasbuig spoke to Tormod Gobha, who nodded to Fearghus Mor. I did not catch what the ground officer said, but I saw the big fellow follow Tormod into the smithy. He came out with a length of timber balanced across his broad shoulder. The timber had a curving cross-piece near the top, and it was no light burden, even for the like of Fearghus Mor, judging by the slow step on him. I wondered how I could have been so slow on the uptake. There was no mistaking that blackened, weathered length of timber. It was the missing part of the keel from the old wreck on the shore. What I had taken to be a cross-piece were twin branching ribs from the keel, sawn short.

Fearghus Mor set the timber down on an old stone mounting block, standing it upright on the block, propped against the wall of the smithy. Mr Ferguson beckoned to the keepers guarding Mata. They hurried him across to the block and stood him with his back to the timber. The branching ribs were just above the level of his shoulders; two black arms curving out on either side of him.

The forge was roaring, glowing red, a shimmer of sparks flying. Tormod Gobha had a piece of iron in his tongs at the face of the anvil, busy drawing it to a point with quick blows of his hammer. As I watched, he put a point on the other end, then bent the iron round into a U-shape on the horn of the anvil. There was the hiss of hot iron, as he plunged the finished staple into a pail of water, and turned back to the forge.

Not a sound came from the crowd, not the least murmur. The black stallion was throwing his small head about, blowing through his wide, open nostrils. The factor's gloved hand stroked the pony's neck, gently as the hand of a mother soothing a restless child. There was a sudden quiet stir in the crowd, like the first little flurry of wind after the dawn calm. Tormod Gobha was making for the group around Mata, hammer in hand.

Fearghus Mor and another of the keepers seized Mata's wrists, and spread his arms wide, forcing them back along the curving span of the ribs. Tormod Gobha dipped into the big pocket of his apron, drew out one of the iron staples he had made, and hammered it into the wood, shackling Mata's left wrist to the timber. He crossed to his other side, where Fearghus Mor had the tinker's right arm spread wide, and hammered a second staple home. As the blacksmith stepped back, the keepers pulled Mata forward, so that the heavy timber scraped clear of the block, and he was bearing its weight entire.

The factor dismounted, leading the pony by the bridle. He put a hand up to each of the staples in turn, and spoke sharply to the smith. Tormod Gobha had to get to work again with his hammer before the factor was satisfied. He mounted his pony, and said to Gilleasbuig, 'Tell the tinker he is free to go.'

'You can make off, old man,' Gilleasbuig said. 'You have a long march before you. The last I heard o' your tribe they were over the hill and camped at Raisaburgh.'

Bent low to take the weight, his shackled arms outflung, Mata started forward, the heavy black keel from the old wreck bearing down on his back as if it would force him to the ground. The crowd parted slowly to make way for him, the only sound the strange grunting noises coming from the throat of Seoras the deaf mute, and himself not knowing he was making them, poor dummy.

I never thought Mata had the strength in him to bear the weight of that waterlogged keel, let alone walk with it on his back. But he got through the crowd, and kept on past the mill where the track took a long curve, joining the road as it came down to the bridge across the Conon.

The factor was the first to make off, and the crowd parted quicker for him. They had to, if they were not to be ridden down. He gave the pony his head, and the black stallion spread his legs, bursting through the crowd, and breaking into such a gallop it was a wonder to me that the wind of his passing did not make Mata stumble and fall.

The men showed no sign of moving, milling around in ever-changing groups, a buzz of talk on the go now that the factor was no longer there. They put me in mind of a crowd at the horse fair gathered to watch a wild colt being haltered, all eyes on the beast, but turning their backs once it was brought down and broken to a rope around its neck. The most of them would end up in the taproom of the inn, joking about the smart way the factor had sorted the tinker.

I saw Tomas Caogach and Fearghus Mor on either side of Mr Ferguson, listening respectfully to the Head Keeper laying off his chest. Murchadh the Marag, the fat son of the big fellow, was at the head of a bunch of boys trailing along behind Mata; the Marag capering and dancing, clown that he was. I clambered down from my perch in the tree, trying to hold my back in from the touch of my shirt, and made after them as fast as I was able.

I kept behind them for fear that Mata might somehow manage to turn his head and catch a sight of me. They followed him to the road and across the bridge over the Conon, past the long white house of Mr Ferguson that was the factor's in the days when a laird stayed at the Lodge; past the Established Church, a small place, not half the size of our kirk; past the tacksman's big house with its twelve brown chimney pots; past the short bridge over the deep bed of the Rha, moving on to the start of the long, slow climb that did not stop until the high moor was reached; past the shoemaker's hut, thinking to myself that old Seumas was one I had not seen in the crowd at the smithy; past the merchant's shop, the door bolted and barred against custom, for a wonder: and all the time Mata plodding on, arms shackled to his burden, back bent under the heavy keel, a black scarecrow creeping slowly up the long hill.

It was when he plodded past the track leading down to our township — one last straight climb ahead before the road twisted and turned to break out from the hill into the waste of high moor — that the mischief started. It happened so quick, I suppose I should not swear to it, but even though I were blind of an eye I would take an oath that it was the Marag who threw the first stone. Then they were all at it, scrabbling for stones at the roadside, hurling them at Mata, and it that dark all of a sudden it might have been a shadow on the road they were stoning, and not a living man at all.

'Let him be,' I shouted at the top of my voice, 'Let him be.' But not one of them took a blind bit of notice, caught up in the kind of Hallowe'en madness that comes when a pack of guisers is on the prowl looking for sport.

The Marag was up on the bank above our township, heaving at a monster of a boulder that he could not get clear of the ground, Tormod Beag and Niall grubbing for stones beside him. I rushed up the bank and caught his ankle with one hand and gave him a sharp push in the back with the other. The Marag let out a strangled shriek as he flew through the air, and if he did not roll far enough to reach old Mairi Beathag's midden, I was not to blame. Tormod Beag got a grip on my shoulder. The pain went through me like a hot knife. I swung round, lashing out blindly at him. My fist struck him full on the nose. He let go of my shoulder, clasping both hands to his face to stem the spouting blood.

Niall set up a chant, 'Calum Og's a tinker! Calum Og's a tinker!' and they all took it up, the whole pack turning on me, Mata forgotten. I went down under a rush of bodies, kicking and striking out in vain. They had me by the legs and arms, and were about to throw me down the bank — calling to the Marag, who was letting out terrible swears below, to keep clear — when there was a clap of thunder fit to split the world apart.

The thunder rolled and cracked around the hills, and before the last echo had died away a great flash of jagged lightning ripped open the sky, turning night into bright day. The boys

70

froze. I saw their faces above me, pale in the lightning's flash — jaws agape, eyes wide. They were not any more scared than me.

There was another great roaring clap of thunder, directly overhead. They did not wait for the lightning to come. Dropping me at their feet, they scattered and ran.

10

I was on my knees, painfully pushing myself up, when the second flash of lightning blazed before my eyes, destroying the darkness in a fierce, forked thrust that tore the sky apart. I crouched down again, thinking of the blackened rock at the back of our peat bog — and it much the same size as me — split clean asunder where lightning had once struck. The long straight of the empty road was lit clear, brighter than day, all the way up to the rocky peak where the road swung sharp to the right, and started the steep zigzag climb round the high crags to the open moor.

The splintered sky became whole again. It was dark once more; a safe, beautiful dark. I wondered if the lightning had struck a faint spark of life in the dead eyes of the *Ceistear*; if a grey glimmer of that dazzling white light had penetrated his darkness. Or had he not so much as blinked an eye, all unknowing that night was turned into day? You would think the blinded would be able to *feel* a light so fierce. It seemed to me that a thousand candles burning bright every yard of the way could not have lit the empty road more clear.

The empty road!

I got to my feet, shouting, 'Mata! Mata! Where are you, Mata?' But the words were snatched from my lips before they gained substance, swept away in a crashing peal of thunder that rolled around the hills, and went on booming and echoing as if the noise would never cease. And before the thunder was spent, the rain came, sheeting down from the heavens in a solid wall of water. I put my head down and ran straight across the road, taking the side drain in my stride and scrambling up the steep face of the hill to the dark outcrop of rock that marked the entrance to *Uamh an Oir*. Another lightning flash lit the hillside. Under the dark outcrop of bare rock, the low opening of the cave flickered and gleamed like a golden eye.

I stopped dead in my tracks, heedless of the drenching rain, petrified by the sight of that winking golden eye. It was dark again, thunder crashing overhead, the golden eye gone. But I made no move. I stood motionless on the open hillside, battered near stupid by the force of the rain, before the answer came to me. It was that simple, I let out a hoarse croak of a laugh to mock my fears. *Uamh an Oir*: the Cave of Gold. I had often wondered how the cave had got its name. Anything less like a cave of gold than that dark hole in the hill you could not imagine. When I was little, and played with the rest of the boys at warring clans, the rocky outcrop was our castle and the cave was always the dungeon where we held our prisoners. I had not been frightened of it then, and now that I was up in years and done with childish things it was a piece of nonsense to let the lightning put a scare on me. With the sky dark again, there was no gleam of gold from the opening. The winking golden eye that had brought me to a stop was a trick of light, a reflection drawn in the lightning's dazzling flash from the bare rock face inside the cave. Someone seeking shelter from a bad thunderstorm long ago — that long ago even the old men had no mind of it — had seen that same queer trick of light, and given the cave its name.

I was suddenly aware that I was soaked to the skin, shivering like one bad with the fever. I ran on up the hill, and ducked inside the low opening of the cave, out of the rain that was falling as if the flood of waters was come again upon the earth.

It was the fiercest thunderstorm that I had ever seen. There was no slow abatement of the thunder, no gradual easing of the lightning, as the storm moved out to sea. There was no moving out to sea at all. The thunderstorm stayed fast above the bay, and it stopped — thunder, lightning and rain — as suddenly as it had begun. With the sudden quiet, the air was full of the sound of running water, coursing fast down the beds of streams that had been dry since the good weather came in May.

My back seemed to be on fire under the sodden shirt, that sore I could no more straighten myself fully upright than fly. So much for the *cailleach* and her Moonseed Bitters made special for the gentry. More like, the packman had made the ointment himself from the fat of a braxy sheep — he was fit for it, the same one. I poked my head out of the cave, and sniffed the air. It was fresh and sweet, like the beginning of a split-new day, the stifling heat banished entire. The sky was lightening fast, only broken trails of ragged clouds left in the west. I took a slow, zigzag course down to the road, stepping as careful as any old man hard stricken in years. As I reached the road, a pale half moon hoisted herself over the hill. The moon lit the bay, peaceful as if the storm had never been.

I trotted up the road and round the sharp bend to the right, the peak of the rock face black above me, expecting to come upon Mata around the next bend in the road. He was hardy, right enough, that was easy seen the way he had plodded on, never faltering, with that terrible weight of timber bearing down on his back. He must have kept going right through the storm, and there was not a man in the place with the nerve on him for the like of that. Imagine footing it out round the crags, through thunder and lightning and a flood of rain, shackled to a load that would have daunted an ox. If that had been Tomas Caogach he would have been down on his knees — and not just from the weight of timber on his back. And he was the one whose lip had curled in contempt, who had spat out the word *tinker* as if it was an abomination to his tongue.

I trotted on, certain sure that I would find Mata around the next turn in the road, only to discover when I rounded the bend that the stretch before me was as empty as the one I had left. My sense told me that not even Fearghus Mor — and himself as strong as a bull — could have reached this length, not in the face of the storm that had raged. But I kept on, not wanting to listen to sense, until I had lost count of the twists and turns in the road. Then, at last, I was out on the high moor, the sky clear above, the road stretching out as far as the eye could see empty under the moon. Mata had vanished.

I walked back, stopping to peer into every dark patch of shadow under the lee of the hill, for fear he had stumbled and fallen and could not rise under the weight of his burden. Down the way, the road twisting and turning round the crags; wheeling sharp left under the rock face, and down the long straight; past the old stone quarry; past the boulder on the bank where I had sent the Marag flying, and the rest of them had turned on me; on to the track that led down to our township.

I was that weary and down in the mouth my feet started to turn for home of their own accord. A new thought leapt unbidden into life, bringing fresh hope. I stopped. What about the quarry? Mata must have been close to the quarry when the stoning started. Supposing he had sheltered there while the storm raged? He could be there still, resting, gathering his strength for the long tramp across the hill to the tents of his tribe. I ran back up the road, weariness forgotten, and burst into the quarry calling, 'Mata! Are you there, Mata!'

I saw the soles of his feet first, naked as skinned rabbits, heels uppermost, sticking out from under the ragged ends of his trousers. The timber from the keel of the old wreck had found water again; half of it was sunk in a pool under the quarry face. Mata lay under the timber, his head down in the water. I splashed into the pool, and got my hands under the curving wooden ribs that held his arms, and dragged him clear, pulling him over so that he lay on his back on the quarry floor. I got down on my knees, and took a hold of his face between my hands. His face was like ice. A shred of tobacco clung to his beard. I plucked it free, and it fell from my fingers into the pool. I watched the tobacco floating on the water for long enough before the tears came. Mata was dead. I had known that the moment I clapped eyes on his feet, but it was the sight of that shred of tobacco floating on the pool that brought the tears to my eyes.

I do not know how long I knelt beside him, weeping like a girl. Even when I was done weeping, I did not get up and go. It seemed wrong to leave him lying there, shackled fast to the timber, his arms spread wide to the cold moon. I thought to try to ease his hands through the staples until I saw the ridged flesh swollen against the irons. The staples had been hammered home until they were hard against his wrists. It would need a saw at the irons before Mata's body was rid of its burden, and the marks of the fetters on his wrists would still be there when they buried him.

I waited until a wisp of cloud had tangled the moon, and his face was in shadow, before I got up and left him.

The busy click-click-click of the *cailleach's* bone knitting pins — pins that I thought kept going of their own accord — halted the moment I stepped inside the door. 'What kept you, boy?' she cried. 'You will get your death prowling in the night air, and you soaked to the skin. Have you no — .'

Trust her to notice the state of my trousers and shirt before lifting her eyes to my face. But when she saw me aright, the words died on her. Her gaze swung to Tomas Caogach and Fearghus Mor, the pair of them side by side on the bench, and themselves the ones I had my eyes on. 'You have killed Mata,' I said, 'you two and Mr Ferguson and the factor, you have killed Mata the tinker.'

'That boy is not wise,' Fearghus Mor bellowed. 'As sure as I am here, that boy is not wise.'

'He is dead,' I said, 'in the old stone quarry, and the pair o' you the ones that gave him over to the factor and killed him.'

'Dead?' Fearghus Mor said. 'The tinker? And him stepping out lively for all the load on his back. Dead?' He gave a snort.

'Never the day. A tinker does not die that easy, more's the pity. You have heard of a cat and the lives it has? Well, a tinker could give a cat nine lives — aye, and more — and still be going strong when the poor cat is stretched out stiff and cold.'

'It is Mata that is stretched out stiff and cold,' I said, 'and it is you that killed him.'

They all started talking at once.

Fearghus Mor: 'Away!'

The *cailleach*: 'What kind o' nonsense is this?'

Tomas Caogach, strangely slow to find his tongue: 'Is this you up to one o' your tricks, boy?'

Fearghus Mor again: 'Amn't I after telling you that boy is not wise? There are poor craturs away in the District Asylum not half so far gone as that one.'

I was far gone right enough — with rage. I could not stop myself from trembling, and as fast as I blinked them away the tears sprang back to my eyes. If only I had been able, I would have felled Fearghus Mor with one blow at that great jutting jaw of his. 'Not wise, am I?' I fairly spat at him. 'Since when did you need to be wise to lift a man from a pool and know he is not living? Wait you, until you have laid eyes on the body yourself — you will not laugh so quick then.'

I marched to the door and flung it open, and stood there waiting for them to follow. They took their time about it, but they came, Tomas Caogach stopping at the door to say to my mother, who was close on his heels, 'Keep to the house, woman. This is no time o' night for you to be out gallivanting.'

She obeyed him, but she did not go inside. She stood at the door watching us, as I hurried ahead of them on the way to the quarry.

The wisps of cloud had come together and multiplied, misting the moon. I waited for the pair of them at the entrance to the quarry, and pointed to the dark shape by the pool in the hollow under the face. 'There he is,' I said.

Fearghus Mor led the way, striding fast, that eager to see you would have thought it was a hoard of gold sovereigns I had found, not a dead man. The two of them squatted down beside the body. Once I had summoned my courage, I went after them. To tell the truth, I had no fancy to look upon the dead face of Mata again. As I came up behind them, Fearghus Mor rose to his feet, and struck me a backhanded blow across the side of the head that sat me down in the pool with a splash. I was slow in getting out of the wet, half stunned by the force of the blow, my head fairly ringing. But when he reached down to grab me by the shoulder I was quick enough to dart away, fearful of the weight of his big hand on my aching back. 'Come you here, boy,' he said. 'I will not lay a finger on you, I promise. Come you here, and look.'

I edged forward warily, but he stepped back so that I had a clear view. At that moment the moon shook herself free of cloud, and shone down on the quarry floor. The timber of the old keel lay where I had dragged it clear of the pool, the black arms of the curving ribs spread wide — like Mata's outflung arms, I thought stupidly. But there was no Mata, no body shackled to the timber. Mata had gone.

I could not have uttered a word supposing my life depended on it. I gaped down at the timber from the old wreck, my mind in a whirl. The rib nearest the quarry face rested athwart a flat stone, exactly the way it had lain when I took my leave of Mata. But Mata was gone.

'There is your dead tinker, boy,' Fearghus Mor crowed, kicking at the barnacle crusted keel. 'That one has been dead many a long year — part o' the keel of the old wreck that has lain on the shore since the year o' the great gale when I was just a boy, near your age.'

I could only stand there and gape, the power of speech gone from me entire.

'What wi' the shadows, the keel had the look of a body to me,' Tomas Caogach said. 'When I first got a sight o' them ribs sticking out like arms, I could have sworn it was the tinker.'

'That is what the boy was seeing,' Fearghus Mor chortled, his good humour restored now that he had proved himself right to his own satisfaction. 'He got a sight o' the keel wi' the ribs stuck out,' — He spread his own arms wide from the thick trunk of his body — 'and that was him off like the wind.' He gave me a dunt in the ribs, and let out a bellow of laughter. 'The next time you fancy you are seeing a dead man,' he said, very near choking he was laughing that much, 'be sure you creep up within spitting distance of him, else every drunkard from the inn that cannot keep his feet is in danger o' being reported dead.'

He gave himself over to laughing, and even Tomas Caogach permitted himself the treat of a dry chuckle. I stood there between the two of them, my head bowed, struck dumb.

What could I say?

That I had hauled him from the pool, and laid him down on his back?

That I had held his icy face between my hands?

That I had plucked a shred of tobacco from his beard?

That I had seen the marks on his wrists where the irons had bit deep?

That I had knelt and wept over him until I was dry of tears?

Fearghus Mor would let fly his great stupid roar of a laugh at me. Or, worse still, say that the place for the likes of me was a barred cell in the District Asylum in Inverness — and maybe have Tomas Caogach believing him.

I got down on my knees, and peered closely at each of the iron staples in the ribs. Neither of them had been prised open by as much as a whisker. They were driven that deep into the timber it was a wonder to me that there was room even for wrists as thin as Mata's. 'How did he make off?' I said, finding my voice at last, 'and the irons there secure in the wood, and not space for a midget of a boy to get his hands free, let alone a grown man.'

'Was there ever a one so thrawn?' Fearghus Mor cried, turning to Tomas Caogach for confirmation. 'He beats me, that boy. He would make out black was white supposing he was blinded and had only his nose to go by, and an army o' sighted men at his back swearing on the Book that he had got it wrong.' He turned on me. 'Listen to me, boy, if you are able. The tinkers are not like us, they are different altogether, that fly you have no idea. They talk o' monkeys having the tricks o' the devil. Not at all. The monkey was not born that has half the tricks o' the tinker. Listen, I mind once, years ago, there was a tinker at the horse fair up in Portree they put chains on. For money. It was a show, see, the tinker was making plenty money at it. Well, it was me that fastened his wrists, and I am telling you I had him chained that tight you would have sworn he would never get free. Mind you, it was not on his feet he was at the escaping, not at all. He was put in a big wool bag, and hung from a beam. Upside down, mind. Well, the bold fellow had the chains off o' him, and was out o' that bag quicker than I could take a lace out o' my boot. It was a trick, see. They were saying he had the knack of swelling his wrists up before the chains were put on, so that he could slip them no bother once he was in the bag. Oh, they are fly, the tinkers. There is no knowing the tricks they get up to.'

'Who knows?' Tomas Caogach said. 'The rest o' the tribe may have come creeping back for that Mata.'

'Well, they did not find him dead, that is a sure thing,' Fearghus Mor said. He gave his bellow of a laugh. 'If they had come on the old one dead, it is his body they would have left behind, not that good timber.'

Tomas Caogach toed the keel gently. 'Aye, it is a rare piece o' timber,' he allowed. 'Good Scots oak. The best just. And not a trace o' rot in her.'

'You could not wish for better,' the big fellow said.

'A pity to leave it lying, and the factor bound to hear,' Tomas Caogach said.

'Hear what?' Fearghus Mor asked him.

'That the tinker made off so easy.'

'There is no knowing wi' tinkers, they are that fly.'

'Aye, but the factor thought he had him. You know fine, Fearghus, the factor would not be pleased if he found the tinker had shed his load before he was out o' sight of the Lodge.'

'Pity the one who has to take the tale to him. I would not fancy the job.'

'The factor need never know supposing the timber is not left to tell the tale. Nobody would be any the wiser if you made off with it now.'

They talked about tinkers being fly. But there was none so fly as Tomas Caogach. He had planted the seed in Fearghus Mor's mind, and the big fellow too slow to see that my uncle held him hostage if he made off with timber belonging to the factor. Likely, Tomas Caogach was wanting to make double-sure that no word would ever spill from Fearghus Mor's lips about the nephew of the elder caught lying naked by the river on the Sabbath. But the big fellow had no word of that; his greed for the timber got the better of him. 'I will make down to the byre with it right off,' he said, grunting as he lifted the keel, and hefted it across his broad shoulder. 'But there must be no word o' this from you, boy.'

'Not him,' Tomas Caogach said, answering for me. 'He will want to sing dumb about the body that was never there.'

Many a night I thought of Tomas Caogach's words, sitting up in bed, gasping for breath, drenched in sweat. I sang dumb, as he had said I would. Not even Marsali heard from me what I had seen in the old stone quarry. Indeed, I sang dumb to my own self, afraid to ask myself a single question for fear the truth could not be contained within the safe prison of my mind. But I could not shut out sleep, and the dreams that came with sleep.

79

Every night I dreamed the same dream. Every night I found myself bolt upright in bed, fighting for breath, my shirt soaked in sweat. In my dream, I saw a pair of arms spread wide, shackled to tar-blackened timbers. I never saw the body or the face, only the arms. And the wrists always came close to my eyes, so that I could see the way they were hard pressed against the unyielding timber, and trace the course of the angry ridged swelling where the irons bit into the flesh. That fierce grip of the irons on the thin brown wrists was always the last vision to come to me before I awoke in a sweat.

That same dream haunted my sleep every night throughout the month of July, and it stayed with me into August. I began to believe that I would never be rid of it. The dream was as constant as the weather, such weather that even the old men had to admit they had never seen the like before. It was not just the days of wind and rain that followed the night of the storm. Gales were never absent from the place for long, summer or winter, and rain was no stranger to our island at any time of year. We were too well acquaint with the wind and the wet for that to put us up or down: it was something different altogether that made the weather so queer. It was the way the sun hid himself, and vanished entire from our sight. Day after day, week after week, heavy grey clouds hung low over the bay.

At the end of the first week without a sight of the sun, old Mairi Beathag — and herself a right witch, if looks were a guide, what with her wild white hair hanging all over her wrinkled face, and the way she had of talking to herself, and sucking in her mouth on her toothless gums, and suddenly going off into a mad cackle of laughter — put the story about that the tinker had set a curse on the place, and we would never see the sun again.

'Not ever?' they teased her.

'Not ever,' Mairi Beathag said, 'unless you mend your wicked ways, and make the sun welcome.' And that was a laugh seeing she was the one who shouted after the *Ceistear* whenever she laid eyes on him, miscalling him something terrible, and never went near the kirk.

Seumas the shoemaker said that one good curse from the like of old Mairi Beathag would put to flight the frail curse of a tinker quicker than he could drive a tack through a thin leather sole; and Seumas's saying did the rounds, and got a good laugh whenever it was told. But after twenty days had passed without a blink of sun there was no more laughing; and when August came,

80

and the grey clouds still clung fast to the hill, even the shoemaker forbore to make mock of Mairi Beathag.

It was as if a blight had come upon us. With the lack of sun, there was no growing at all. The cattle roamed the length and breadth of the black moor, searching in vain for fresh shoots of heather and grass. They were a sorry sight, I am telling you. I never saw beasts in such poor trim, lean as at the end of a long, hard winter, no shine at all on their matted coats. A good score of the cows went dry, and the *cailleachs* were not slow to echo Mairi Beathag and say the tinker had put the evil eye on the beasts. For sure, there was not a house in the township with milk to spare for the table. Indeed, we all had little enough to nourish the ailing calves.

It was the same with the crops. The old men said the corn would not be worth the labour of cutting and lifting, even supposing the sun returned in time to ripen the grain before the first bad gales of autumn laid it flat to the ground. It was a misery to look upon, that poor and thin and stunted, no ears on the corn worth the name. Only the patches of thistles — and there were plenty of them — seemed to thrive, and grow big and strong. The potatoes were in every bit as bad a shape, the shaws slowly blackening, row upon withered row of them, dismal heralds of a winter without food. All the talk was of the year of the great hunger when the crops failed, and the people were that desperate for a bite they bled their cattle beasts for food, mixing the blood with the little oatmeal that the women managed to scrape from their empty meal chests.

The only bright spot for me in those sunless days was the absence of the laird's cousin. According to Marsali, she was being entertained by the gentry friends of the laird in their big houses at Vaternish and Dunvegan and Armadale, and folk there enjoying great weather — that was the tale of the packman when he came to our township. I did not grudge the laird's cousin the sun, thankful that she had forgotten me, and the words that could have cost me dear.

That was the way it was with us after the night of the storm, the cattle and the crops failing before our eyes. The terrible spell of weather lasted into the third week of August. I mind well when we first saw the sun again, and I ceased being plagued by the dream. It was the day the stranger came to our township.

11

It was the fiftieth day since the night of the storm — seven long weeks shut fast in a prison of thick cloud — and you have no idea the lift it gave us to be suddenly free of that lowering grey cloud. Tomas Caogach was the first in the house to waken and see that the cloud had gone and the sun was returned in all his glory. I heard him shout — his voice as happy and excited as that of a young boy coming fresh on a new wonder — 'Iseabal! Calum Og! Up and see, the sun is back.'

He burst into the kitchen, and he was a comical sight I am telling you, his long shirt-tails flapping about his bare shanks. He had a grip on the door-latch before he remembered the trousers bundled under his left arm. He gave a laugh — as I am here, Tomas Caogach gave a laugh! — and struggled into his trousers, getting a leg stuck in his haste to drag them on, and very near measuring his length on the floor. He flung the door open, and was away down the croft, barefoot and bare-headed, as eager to be out as a stirk straining to get his first taste of the living green world beyond the gloom of a cramped byre stall.

In all the days of my life, I had never seen Tomas Caogach put his nose out of doors without first pulling on, and lacing tight, his big tackety boots, and taking down his bonnet from the peg on the back of the door and carefully arranging it dead square on his head, every movement — including his progression out of doors — made without haste, as slow and ordered as a yoked ox. And it was not just Tomas Caogach who was acting queer. I had never before heard the *cailleach* humming a song, or seen her with her hair hanging free at her shoulders, as she kindled the fire into fresh life and set about preparing the porridge. She was the one who did not consider herself properly dressed for the work of the house until she had scraped her hair into a bun, and it was scolding, not singing, that came easy to her first thing.

I stood outside the door, halted in my tracks by the bright glitter of the loch, the tide near full, the deep sweep of the bay a brimming blue. The weathered rock faces of the towering headlands were etched that sharp in the clear air I felt I had only to reach out to be able to touch them. I suppose I was seeing the place anew, with eyes as fresh as those of the laird's cousin, who had gazed about her and named the bay beautiful.

My mother came up behind me, and laid a hand on my shoulder. 'It puts me in mind o' summer mornings up the glen in the old days,' she said, 'everything all a-glitter in the sun. We had great summers up the glen in the old days, not like now. You clean forgot even the worst o' winters once the long summer was come, the land fairly baking in the heat, the bees that heavy laden wi' pollen they could scarce fly.'

Hearing her speak of the glen like that, she who never uttered a word about the old days, I wondered if there was magic in the sun's warm glow, a magic strong enough to smooth the sour, drooping lines from her face and make it a fit match for the soft dreamy voice at my back. I was afraid to look, but I had to know, so I chanced a quick glance at her. She was gazing up at the green cleft in the hill beyond the wooded slopes that marked the start of the glen, the sour look gone entire, an eagerness in her face that I had never seen before, as new to me as the sight of Tomas Caogach skipping carefree about the kitchen in his shirt-tails. I kept still and waited, not wanting to break the spell. Her hand stayed on my shoulder.

'My mother did not much fancy your father,' she said, her voice that low it was almost as if she was talking to herself. 'The *cailleach*' — and it was a wonder to me hearing her speak of *her* mother as 'the *cailleach*', as if the burden of years had been lifted from her and she was suddenly young again, no older than Marsali — 'was not pleased at me going about with him. She made out he was too wild a boy for me, and forbade him the house. The *cailleach's* word had always been law. To me. Not to Domhnull Ban, though. And when I was with him I was every bit as bad as himself. I had no word of her either.

'We used to meet under the big willow down by the river below Calum Ban's house — Calum Ban, your grandfather, that died the year before we were cleared from the glen. It was like a green cave under the willow in the summertime. I mind a wee bird used to fly down and perch on a flat rock in the river. He would take a drink and lift his head up to the sun, like he was offering thanks, before he dipped down again for another sip o' water. Domhnull Ban said the bird was a young ring-ousel. We used to sit quiet under the willow and watch him, he was that dainty at his drinking. It is queer the things you mind long years after.'

In the silence between us, close-linked by her hand on my shoulder, I heard myself say, 'Would you have flitted to America if our father had been able to make back for us?'

'It was bad enough leaving the glen for this place down on the shore,' she said, 'never mind making off the length of America.' Her hand left my shoulder and strayed to the back of her neck, puzzled, I think, to find there was no fraying bun to work at. 'I was always the timid one,' she said, clasping her hands in front of her, 'but Domhnull Ban had nerve enough for the two of us, and I was not worrying so long as he was there. Yes, I would have taken you and Marsali and gone to America with him.' She tried a laugh; it sounded more like a sob to me. 'I would ha' gone right enough, and been certain sure the ship was bound for the bottom o' the deep.'

She had not been like Marsali when she was young, I could see that now, and I did not know what to say. She had been softer than Marsali when she was young, the *cailleach*, altogether more timorous, and that was a wonder greater to me than any under the sun.

Tomas Caogach came out of the byre, gazing up at the blue sky, looking that pleased with himself I thought he could not have noticed that he had trodden in cow dung. But he had seen the clinging dung on his heel, and it did not put him up or down. 'It is a beauty of a day,' he said, carefully rubbing his bare feet clean on the grass. 'Is it not a beauty of a day, Calum Og?'

I mumbled that it was, that taken aback I could hardly get the words out, wondering what had come over him that he should take such open delight in the day, and find pleasure in gaining confirmation from me.

'I never saw the sun so bright since years,' my mother said, 'not since the old days up the glen when we were young, Tomas.' She led the way into the house, humming to herself.

I followed them indoors, thinking there must be something special about a sun that had warmed the *cailleach* and Tomas Caogach into happy life, not knowing that the stranger was near and others would change as quick.

The first thing I saw when I came out of the house after breakfast was the coal boat creeping round the headland of Ru Idrigil. There was not a breath of wind on shore, and as the three-masted schooner gained the full shelter of the bay she lost what little wind there was out on the open loch and her brown sails went slack on her, lifeless in the dead calm. A voice carried over the water, bawling orders. That would be the skipper of the schooner, a grumpy old man from the Isle of Mull who had been at the whaling in his young days. He would not be pleased if they did not get his ship beached soon after high water so that no time was lost at the unloading. The crew fairly jumped to it, getting the ship's dinghy lowered. In no time at all, they had the schooner in tow, four of them pulling strong at the oars, striving to beach her before the tide had fallen far.

I wondered if Aindrea Ruadh was one of the four at the oars. Aindrea was a first cousin of Tomas Caogach, and he had sailed with the Mull skipper since the day the old man had come home from the whaling and bought the schooner with his savings. But although they put in with coals for the factor every summer, Aindrea Ruadh never came near the house. He knew my uncle too well to attempt to show face. The sight of the coal boat in the bay was enough to start Tomas Caogach miscalling his cousin, and all because Aindrea liked a laugh and a joke and took a dram with the rest of the crew.

Folk were out at their doors watching the schooner being towed into shore, the dripping oars sparkling in the sun every time the rowers bent their backs and lifted their blades clear of the water. Even old Mairi Beathag was still and silent for once, as she stood at her door gazing out over the bay at the slowly moving ship.

I saw Raonull, Tormod Beag's father, climb the turf dyke that marked the boundary between our crofts, and I did not fancy the way he squared his shoulders as he made over to the house. There was bad blood between himself and Tomas Caogach. Last January a wild stirk of Raonull's had broken into our stackyard late one night, and created havoc, pulling whole sheaves clear of the corn stack and trampling them underfoot in his greed to get at a bite. Tomas Caogach had come upon the beast in the morning, and laid into him with his stick, and chased him down the croft. The stirk leapt the dyke and landed in the big drain, where he stuck fast, sinking slowly, only his head clear of the water. It had taken all the men in the township to haul the beast out of the drain, and Raonull and Tomas Caogach had never spoken a word to each other from that day on. We heard that Raonull was saying Tomas Caogach was that jealous of his good beasts he had tried to drown his best stirk, and I do not doubt that word reached Raonull that Tomas Caogach was making out he was that short of fodder he had taken to putting his beasts out on the sly at night, knowing fine they were that desperate for a bite they would raid other folk's stackyards.

Raonull walked right by me as if I had not been there, and stuck out his hand to Tomas Caogach, who was standing bent in the doorway, my mother close at his back. The pair of them shook hands, like any two friends coming together who have not seen each other for a week or two. 'Well, Tomas,' Raonull said, as if there had never been a cross word between them, 'the factor has got a great day for the landing of his coals. I mind the first time the old schooner ever put in wi' a cargo — and that was not yesterday — and you and me made down from the glen to watch her unload.'

'I mind that fine, Raonull,' Tomas Caogach said, the long, frozen silence between them broken as easy as if it had been no more than the pause taken to light a pipe, 'and it a day the dead spit o' this one.'

They fell to talking, and I watched Tormod Beag, Niall, Ruairidh and Alasdair Ruadh as they raced down Fearghus Mor's croft, Murchadh the Marag labouring along at their back, calling on them to wait for him. Rob and Aonghas and Lachlann were all making down to the shore from different directions. Seoras the dummy was up and over the turf dyke at the foot of his father's croft, swift as a deer in flight. Seoras was going to be the first to reach the water's edge.

'Why are you not off wi' the others?' my mother said, and it was not like her to urge me to make off on idle play with the boys when there was work to be done — the cattle haltered in their stalls, and it my job to put them out to the common grazing on the hill.

'Aye, away you go wi' the rest o' the boys,' Tomas Caogach said. 'I will put out the cattle. And if Aindrea Ruadh is wi' the coal boat still tell him I said he was to show face at the house and take a bite o' supper with us before he is away.'

I was off like a shot before either of them could change their mind, leaping dykes until I came to Fearghus Mor's croft, where I soon overhauled the Marag. I had my hand up ready to slap his great wobbling backside as I sprinted past, but when it came to the bit I did not have the heart to leave him behind. I gave him a pat on the back, and slackened my pace to his own slow trot, and the two of us jogged on side by side to join the crowd on the shore.

Heaving lines were tossed from the deck of the schooner to the men in the dinghy when the ship grounded. They rowed ashore, and hauled in the lines and secured the mooring ropes to big rocks on the shore. A few quick strokes of the oars took them back alongside the schooner. She seemed to be floating still, but her keel was fast in the soft sand. Once the ebb tide had left her, she would settle on her bilge, and the unloading would start. The waiting carts would move out to the ship's side, the retreating tide washing about the horses' hooves, and the skipper would chalk up each bucket of coal on the shaft of the weighing-beam before it was emptied into the cart below.

I had seen it all before, but I never tired watching the un-loading of the coal boat. It always came fresh to me the sight of the old schooner lying beached on her side, her black, dripping flanks exposed, helpless as a stranded whale. And I always got the foolish notion that she was slowly dying as the sea left her. Not that it was all that foolish a notion, because you could see her coming back to life as the sea returned, her timbers groaning loud as she shifted with the incoming tide; and it was as if she breathed again as she finally came clear of the shore and floated free. And the old skipper was always good for a laugh, that afraid of missing a tide in his haste to be away he was forever cursing the carters, in his queer Mull Gaelic, for being too slow in coming forward with their carts to the ship's side, and it was comical to see his white tuft of a goat's beard getting blacker and blacker with coal dust as the unloading went on. But this day I never saw the start of the unloading. Indeed, I had my back to the coal boat, watching Rob and the Marag to see which of them would strike the first blow, and when their argument was over it was not the old skipper and his schooner that took my eye.

The argument started the way arguments near always do, over nothing at all, Aonghas wanting to know why the factor took home coals instead of cutting peats like everyone else in the place. But the Marag had to make out that he knew more about the gentry than the rest of us, and Rob was not the one to suffer the like of that in silence.

'The gentry have no fancy at all for peats,' the Marag declared. 'My father has been about big houses all over the place, and he says it is coals and logs the gentry burn, great roarers o' fires on the go from morn till night in every room – and there are rooms galore in all them big houses – so that a servant is on the hop steady just keeping the fires stoked.'

'It must cost them a fortune wi' coals a half sovereign a ton,' Rob said.

'How do you know the price o' coals?' the Marag demanded.

'Old Seumas told me,' Rob said. 'Old Seumas knows all about the price o' coals, and many a thing besides. He reads newspapers, the same one. He has *The Highlander* brought home special by the mail coach.'

That shut up the Marag. There was not a scholar in the place the equal of the shoemaker, and himself a stranger to schooling.

'Imagine paying a half sovereign for a ton o' coals!' Tormod Beag exclaimed.

'Where does the factor get all that money from?' Aonghas asked.

'The factor is not doing the paying, you clown,' Niall said. 'It is the laird that pays.'

'The laird, then,' Aonghas said.'

'The laird has pots o' money,' Tormod Beag said.

'No wonder,' Rob said, 'seeing the rents he is raking in.'

'That is where you are wrong, boy,' the Marag declared, thrusting his chin out the way Fearghus Mor did when he was wild. 'The rents are neither here nor there when it comes to the bit.'

'How not?' Rob wanted to know.

'It is easy seen you are pig ignorant about the gentry,' the Marag sneered. 'The gentry have their own money.'

'Aye, from the big rents they are after charging poor folk,' Rob said.

'That is how they can buy tons and tons o' coals,' the Marag swept on unheeding, 'and pay servants to stoke their fires and put folk to work at making roads and digging drains and planting trees and . . .'

'Building kennels o' fancy stone for their dogs,' Rob butted in.

'. . . many a thing besides I cannot just mind of,' the Marag finished, glaring at him. 'It all comes out o' their own money.'

'Where did they get their money?' Rob said, poking a finger in the Marag's chest. 'Tell me that, if you can.'

We had gradually spread out around the two of them, giving them space, in the sure expectation that they would come to blows. Rob's prodding finger looked like the start of the fight, but the Marag just leaned on him, and he had to give ground.

'I will tell you, boy,' the Marag crowed. 'They were left money.'

'Who by?' Rob said.

'Gentry that was there before them,' the Marag said.

'And how did they get money?' Rob said, coming at him again, the prodding finger on the poke.

The Marag pushed him back. 'The same way,' he said. 'They were left money by gentry before *them*. That has always been the way of it. It has always been the gentry that has had the money. That way they can pay folk wages for to work for them. If there was no gentry there would be no work for folk because it is only the gentry that has the money to pay.'

'What about America?' Rob said.

'What about America?'

'There is work in America. Many a one has gone from this place and got work in America.'

'Well?'

'Well there is no gentry in America — no Lords and Ladies and the like.'

'America is different altogether. America went to war against the King.'

'Aye, and cleared out the gentry. But never mind the war. Before the war. At the start.'

'There was gentry then.'

'Never the day. There was Indians just — and ordinary folk.'

'There must ha' been gentry.'

'There was not.'

'There was.'

'There was not.'

'There was.'

They were going at it hammer and tongs, pushing hard at one another now, each of them waiting for the other to strike the first real blow. Seoras the dummy was making excited grunting noises deep in his throat. He was older than the rest of us, Seoras, but with his sharp, pointed face and untidy mop of dark hair and big brown eyes, that were forever flitting anxiously from face to face seeking to understand what was going on, he had the look of a wild, shy thing, poised for flight at the least sound — and himself deaf to the loudest thunderclap.

Seoras was standing across the ring from me, facing the shore, but he was not looking at Rob and the Marag as they circled one another warily in the ring. He was staring over my shoulder, like a man who cannot believe what he sees. I saw him give a tug at Aonghas's arm. Aonghas looked at him, and followed his fixed gaze. His mouth dropped open. 'In the name of creation,' he cried, pointing a trembling finger, 'what kind of a beast is that?'

12

I recognised the beast right off, although I had never seen a real live one before. It was a monkey. There was a picture of one just like him in a book of animals belonging to old Seumas that me and Rob used to look at when we were little. The monkey was perched on the shoulder of a man standing at the water's edge alongside the beached dinghy. He was a man of middle stature, long black hair bushing out from under his peaked seaman's cap. His face was clean-shaven, the tawny hue of his complexion darker than a tinker's. His eyes were darker still. He had the most piercing dark eyes on him that I had ever seen on any man. He was wearing a jacket of sober dark blue homespun, but there was a bright splash of colour at his throat, where a scarf of gaudy calico was caught loosely about his neck. He carried a sailcloth pack slung across his back on a canvas strap, and he was smiling at us, his teeth whiter even than Marsali's in the dark of his face. The little monkey, perched on his left shoulder, regarded us with big, sad eyes.

Aonghas swallowed hard. 'What kind of a beast is it?' he whispered.

'It is a monkey, you clown,' Rob said, all thought of his argument with the Marag forgotten.

'Can it talk?' Aonghas wanted to know.

'Talk?' Rob said, keeping a straight face. 'Wait you, Aonghas, until the monkey starts laying off his chest. He will come out with great big words, real jawbreakers that not even the *Ceistear* could manage. Mind you, this one may not be good at the Gaelic.'

'The monkey will have better Gaelic than the skipper o' the coal boat,' Niall said solemnly. 'Next to Skyemen, they say monkeys speak the best Gaelic in the land.'

'Away!' Aonghas said, glancing around to see how we were taking it, none too sure of himself until Niall burst out laughing and set the rest of us off.

The stranger drew a silver whistle from his pocket, and put it to his lips, and blew a long shrill blast. He set off along the shore, playing a queer kind of tune, no lilt at all to the music, but a something about the strange high pitch of the notes that made you want to hear more. They all started off after him, without so much as a glance at the coal boat, Seoras the dummy the first to move, striding out in front of the rest.

I was left on my own. The first cart trundled across the wet sand to the schooner, the horse splashing through weed-strewn pools. I saw the red head of Aindrea Ruadh bent over the dinghy, and ran to his side. 'Was it yourself put the stranger ashore, Aindrea?' I asked him.

He nodded, busy baling the dinghy with an old tin can.

'Where is he from?'

Aindrea shrugged. 'Who knows? The skipper took him aboard when we were stormbound in Tobermory. He brought us luck wi' the weather, I will say that for him, and kept the old man in a good mood with his tricks.'

'What tricks?'

'Tricks wi' the cards. The Egyptian is a great hand at the card tricks. But don't you be letting on to your uncle. Tomas is terrible set against anything to do wi' playing cards.'

Rob shouted, 'Calum Og, come on!'

'The Egyptian?' I said, not heading Rob. 'Did you say the Egyptian, Aindrea?'

'That was the nickname the cook put on him. A pity the same one is not as handy at the cooking as he is at making up nicknames. Mind you, that fellow has the look of a right Egyptian, and the nickname fairly stuck.'

'You mean he is all the way from Egypt, Aindrea?'

'*Dhia*, no. Egyptians was the name for gypsies in olden days when they were banished from the kingdom under pain o' death. If you came across a gypsy in them days you could finish him off quick,' — He lifted his chin and drew his forefinger across his throat, rolling his eyes so that only the whites showed — 'and there was no word about it.'

'Calum Og!' Rob bawled.

'Aye, coming,' I shouted back. 'Why were the gypsies banished from the kingdom, Aindrea?'

'For being vagabonds just — sturdy beggars — thieves.'

'Is the stranger a gypsy?'

'You are an awful boy for the questions, Calum Og. Away and ask the man yourself.'

'Ask him straight out is he a gypsy?' I said. 'I have not the nerve for that.'

'Nor me,' Aindrea said.

'Aye, but you must have an idea.'

'Not me, boy.' He straightened his back, and gazed down at the can in his hand, as if he was seeing the reflection of the stranger's dark face in the water it held. 'Gypsy? Tinker? Who knows? He is a travelling man o' sorts, I suppose, but I never saw the like o' that fellow in all my days.'

'Are you not done wi' the dinghy, Aindrea?' the skipper roared from the schooner, his voice sounding out above the clatter of coals being shovelled into the big iron bucket.

'The old man is missing the card tricks already,' Aindrea whispered. He gave me a wink, but he dropped the can into the dinghy smartly enough, and hurried off to answer the captain's call.

The stranger and the boys were out of sight, hidden by a rise in the ground, but I could still hear the thin notes of his silver whistle. I ran after the sound, clean forgetting Tomas Caogach's message for his cousin to call, nothing in my head but the queer, shrill music of the Egyptian.

The stranger led the procession — and it growing all the time as boys and girls came running to join us — away from the shore up to a grassy bank overlooking the bay. We sat around in a ring, and watched him open his pack, chatting away all the time, asking this one and that their name, and even the shyest among them answering him freely. He had good Gaelic, not like the old skipper from Mull, and if voices had a colour his was as rich and dark a brown as his face. But it was not a Gaelic that had come to him with his mother's milk; it did not lie *that* easy on his tongue.

He dressed the monkey in scarlet pantaloons and a short green jacket and a green hat with a stiff scarlet plume. The monkey took off his hat and bowed in turn to all the points of the circle. Then he laid his fine plumed hat on the grass beside his master, and danced to the music of the silver whistle, bouncing up and down as if he had springs in his heels. When the dancing was done, he turned somersaults and cartwheels, finishing up by walking round the circle on his hands, and somersaulting to his feet again.

I thought that was the tricks finished, but there were more to come. The monkey put on his hat, and walked round the ring of spectators on his hind legs, holding out his hand. Supposing it had been a crowd up at the horse fair, the little creature would have got a great collection, but with us there was only Rob to hold out a farthing. The monkey snatched the coin out of Rob's hand, and doffed his hat to him. He held the farthing close to his face, turning it over in his thin, clever fingers before bounding across to his master and giving it to him.

The sun had climbed high in the sky, and the carts were busy trundling back and forth between the beached coal boat and the Lodge, but nobody looked up to mark the passage of time or down to the shore to see what was happening there. They all had their eyes glued fast to the monkey, every single one of them, save me. I was watching the monkey's master.

Aindrea Ruadh had said the stranger was a travelling man of sorts, but he was not a tinker, that was a sure thing. You could see that by the way he lay sprawled at his ease on the bank, as if he owned the place, smiling at the oohs and ahs that greeted the antics of his pet. He was too much at ease to be a tinker. Tinkers had learned to be on their guard, to tread wary, always sniffing for trouble, knowing fine that if one man pointed an accusing finger at them — and himself the worst rogue in the place — every hand would be turned against the whole tribe. But there was nothing wary about the smiling stranger; he had the look of a man careless of trouble. I could not see him — him with the gaudy scarf at his throat, bright as a coloured banner — leaping to his feet if the factor rode by, and snatching the cap from his head like the rest of us. And if the factor came on him sprawled on the grass, and himself with no abode for the night, there would be trouble in plenty. I shut my eyes, and prayed that the factor would stay within the walls of the Lodge until the stranger was safely gone from the place.

Rob dug me in the ribs. The Marag was holding out a small flat pebble to the monkey, grinning all over his big fat face. The monkey took the pebble from him, and he let out a great senseless bray of a laugh when the beast obediently doffed his plumed hat to him. But after the beast had taken a good look at the pebble, and turned it over carefully in his hands, he threw it away, smacking his lips together and making angry clucking noises. We all cheered and clapped like mad, excepting the Marag who coloured as red as a turkey cock. The little monkey was that pleased he joined in the clapping himself.

'Good boy, Runag,' the stranger said, and the monkey ran to him, nestling within the curve of his arm, looking up at his master as if waiting to be told what to do next. Suddenly, he scuttled off, bringing shrieks from the girls by breaking through the circle where they were sitting, and bounding up the bank to the road. Some of the boys made to go after him, but the stranger commanded them to stay. The monkey reached the road just as old Mairi Beathag came into view. I expected her to let out a screech, and make off back up the road crying that the devil was come. But the sight of the monkey in his plumed hat and scarlet pantaloons did not put her up or down. Runag took her hand, and the two of them came down the bank together.

They made the queerest looking pair I had ever laid eyes on; the monkey, arrayed in all his finery, leading a scarecrow of an old woman, a man's ragged jacket on her back, her long black skirts tattered and frayed, the worn uppers of her boots split open, her wild white hair hanging about her face. Nobody laughed, not even the Marag. I believe we were all struck dumb at the sight. For sure, amazement was writ plain on every face. But there was no surprise on the face of the stranger. He got to his feet, and hefted his pack, as if all that had gone before had been no more than a waiting for the coming of Mairi Beathag.

Catriona, Alasdair Ruadh's sister, and herself that shy she was dumb before strangers, keeping to the byre all day rather than face folk in the house she did not know, piped up as bold as you please, 'We are not wanting you and Runag to go.'

'There are others that have been waiting, girl,' Mairi Beathag said, speaking calm for a wonder, no mad cackle of laughter bubbling in her throat, 'Waiting since years out o' mind.'

But for all her quiet spoken words it was the same old Mairi Beathag, babbling nonsense that only she could make out. The stranger's piercing dark eyes fastened on her face, and she said no more. 'We will be back,' he said, 'me and Runag.' He looked around the ring of faces, his eyes lighting on everyone in turn. 'When you hear me whistle a tune, will you come running?'

'Aye,' we all chorused, the Marag shouting as loud as anyone there.

The stranger swung Runag up on his shoulder, and raised his hand in salute. We watched him climb the bank with old Mairi Beathag, herself footing it out as lightly as a girl. Nobody spoke until they were out of sight around the bend in the road.

'He might ha' given me back my farthing,' Rob grumbled. 'I only let the monkey have it to see what he would do.'

I got down to the shore late that afternoon, and saw the last of the coals unloaded, and gave Aindrea Ruadh his cousin's message. 'What in the world has come over Tomas?' Aindrea said, 'that he is wanting the like o' me to break bread with him?'

'He is in a great mood,' I said. 'Coming out o' the byre this morning, he stepped straight into a big pat of dung — and himself without boots — but it did not put him up or down.'

'You are not making mock o' me, boy?'

'Never the day! I was to ask you special to make up to the house for a bite. I forgot when I was down this morning, but don't be telling him that, Aindrea.'

'Well, well, what can have come over him?'

'It is the first day we have seen the sun in weeks,' I said. 'He was that eager to get on the croft first thing, he had the door open before he had got his trousers on.'

'I see it now,' Aindrea said. 'Tomas has got a touch o' the sun.' He clapped his hands to his head, and staggered around, rolling his eyes something terrible, the whites seeming huge in his coal-blackened face. 'Sunstroke. Tomas has got the sunstroke, and it has put him clean off his head.'

He was a comic, Aindrea, but he was looking as solemn as the *Ceistear* when I took him into the kitchen, and his face could not have been cleaner if it had been licked by a patient cat. Tomas Caogach gripped his hand as if he would never let go, and the *cailleach* made a great fuss of him. She had a special supper prepared, not our usual meal of plain porridge, but big bowls of good dulse soup, and the table loaded with scones and barley cakes and a dish of fresh-made butter. I do not believe I ever enjoyed a meal more, there was that much talk on the go, and jokes, too, once Aindrea settled in and shed his solemn front. The *cailleach* had her knitting pins out, and the cousins were sitting on the bench, chattering away good style, when I left the house to fetch home the cattle.

I had just got the beasts stalled, and was coming out of the byre, when Rob pounced on me. 'Come quick,' he panted, tugging at my arm, 'the stranger is along wi' old Seumas.'

'I was going down to the shore to see the schooner sail.'

'To pot wi' the schooner. You should see the tricks that monkey is up to. The beast snatched the pipe out of old Seumas's hand, and made off with it. I very near died laughing seeing the monkey sitting up in the rafters puffing away like a little old man. He was fairly taken with Seumas's pipe. The stranger had some job getting him to come down with it.'

As we ran up the track to the road, Rob said proudly, 'I was helping him gather dry heather for the cave.'

'Who?'

'The stranger.'

'What cave?' I said, thinking he might have sought me out earlier so that I, too, could have helped the stranger.

'*Uamh an Oir*,' Rob said.

I glanced up at the hill. The outcrop of rock that marked the entrance to the cave glittered bright now that the sun was low in the west. But once the sun was down it would be thrown into shadow again, dark and gloomy as the night I had sheltered there. 'I would not fancy it,' I said.

'Nor me,' Rob agreed. 'But he seems fine pleased. And the cave is the right place for the monkey. The beast cannot get up to mischief there.'

'I wonder what Mairi Beathag was wanting wi' the stranger?'

'He told me,' Rob said, preening himself at being the only one in the know. 'Mairi Beathag took him home with her, and gave him a feed.' He laughed. 'I reckon Mairi took a fancy to the monkey. He was a great sight, right enough, in his scarlet pantaloons.'

'What is the stranger doing along wi' old Seumas?'

'He just walked in, and the two o' them got cracking away right off. He is not slow at making himself at home, the stranger.' He slowed to a walk, as we neared the shoemaker's hut. 'We will slip in and sit quiet,' he said. 'Watch old Seumas. Every time he takes a puff at his pipe he is squinting up at the rafters for fear the monkey is set to pounce on him.'

Rob stopped at the door of the shoemaker's hut. He dug his hand into his pocket, and held out his open palm to me. 'See,' he whispered. 'The stranger gave me back my farthing.'

Neither of them took the least notice of us as we crept into the hut, they were that deep in talk. Old Seumas was perched on the high stool at his work-bench, leaning forward eagerly laying off his chest, his bald head gleaming; a small man, quick as a bird in his movements, but bent at the shoulders, and that shrunk with age his clothes hung loose about his frame. The stranger sat on an upturned herring barrel, elbows propped on the end of the work-bench, his chin resting on his folded hands as he listened to Seumas. An open copy of *The Highlander* was spread between them, poked into a peak where it rested on a pair of unfinished boots.

'What was different about the old days?' the shoemaker was saying. 'Everything just. People were different. They had time to help one another. Now, they cannot even help themselves, they are that plagued for want of money. There was land in plenty in the old days when we stayed up the glen. Folk were not forced to live off one another's backs. When a man sold his beasts at the Sale, and put by money for the rent, what was left was for himself. Now, it is money for the right to cut peats, money for the right to gather sea-ware, money for to get their corn ground at the mill. I mind the day when peats and sea-ware were there for the taking, and near every house had its own quern. But the laird had a mill built, and folk had to pay for to get their corn ground — and to make sure they took their corn to the mill the ground officer was sent round the houses to break their handmills in pieces.

'And in the old days one bad harvest did not mean empty pots and empty bellies, not so long as the back end o' the year brought the herring shoals into the loch. There was fish for the lifting from the *cairidh* — fish galore — enough to last the winter through, dried and salted; and nothing wasted when we had fish, that was how we got the oil for our lamps. It was a bad day for this place when the factor had the stones o' the *cairidh* cast down.'

He was always on about the *cairidh*, old Seumas, and no wonder if the fishing was half as good as he made out. I think it was the constant sight of the ruin of the fish-trap, very near under his nose, that roused him to anger and made him keep on so. He had only to take a few steps from his hut to be able to gaze down into the clear waters of the bay and see the remains of the great horse-shoe ring of stones that had formed the *cairidh*. It had been built like a drystone dyke, reaching out on the sea beach below the high-water mark. The fish came in on the flood tide, and were trapped inside the wall when the tide ebbed, making an easy haul for the fishers as they waded out with their landing nets.

Seumas's pipe had gone out. He struck a match, squinting up at the rafters as he puffed at his pipe. The monkey was crouched on a beam at the far end of the hut, watching his every move. The beast swung down, hanging by his hands, but he scrambled back to his perch when the stranger brandished his bright silver whistle at him.

'There was great fishing at the *cairidh*,' the shoemaker went on. 'I mind the July we took a hundred salmon on the one tide, and that was a blessing for poor folk wi' salmon fetching up to sixpence a pound from the merchants. And when the herring shoals came swarming up the loch from the sea many's the day in October the trap was just a solid lump o' fish from end to end.'

'Are the stones there still?' the stranger asked, idly spinning the silver whistle between his fingers.

'Aye, but cast down,' Seumas said, 'covered wi' weed and deep in sand the most o' them.'

'Then the *cairidh* could be raised again easy enough,' He smiled his quick, flashing smile. 'I am a good enough hand at drystone walling. How would it be if I tackled the job myself for you?'

'Away!' the shoemaker scoffed. 'It would take months o' labour.'

'Weeks, maybe,' he said quietly.

I do not think old Seumas heard him, not that it would have made any difference if he had. 'And where the *cairidh* reaches far out,' he went on, 'you would be working up to your chest in water, even at the full ebb — and once the tide turns that is you driven ashore again. It is an army o' men you would need for the like o' that job. Besides, the herring are gone from the loch since years.'

'The herring may return,' the stranger said.

'Not a man in this place believes we will ever see the herring again,' Seumas said, 'and not a one o' them would put a toe in the water to make good the old *cairidh*, I can tell you that. So where will you find your army?'

'I will raise an army o' boys, if their fathers are not able,' the stranger said. 'There are two o' them here — see what they say.' His piercing dark eyes shifted from my face to Rob's. 'Would you not give me a hand, boys?'

'Aye, surely,' we chorused as one.

'You are after forgetting the factor,' the shoemaker said. 'One word from the factor and you will not get to lift a single stone.'

The stranger stared at Seumas. 'But what if the factor does not say a word?' He had the whistle at his lips, and I saw his cheeks swell as he blew, but I did not hear the least whisper of a note — and no wonder seeing the sudden wild screech the monkey let out. The beast swung down from the rafters, landing at my feet, the hairs of his coat bristling. Seumas dropped his pipe, and very near fell off his stool snatching at it. But the monkey was not after the shoemaker's pipe. The beast scuttled across the floor, and leapt into the stranger's lap, long arms encircling his neck. The stranger stroked the monkey's head, and spoke softly to him.

'What came over the beast?' Seumas said.

'He must have heard something, and taken fright,' the stranger said. 'Come on, Runag, it is time for you and me to lay down our heads.'

He got to his feet, the monkey clinging tight to him, and raised his hand in salute. As he went out the door, we saw the schooner putting out to sea, her topsails filling as she caught the off-shore breeze, sailing into the crimson glow of the setting sun.

'He is a nice enough fellow for a man on the tramp,' Seumas said, 'but I did not fancy the monkey. Away and boil a kettle o' tea, Rob. I could not stomach the thought o' tea wi' that beast peering down at me from the rafters, and I am as dry as a cork. Build up the *cairidh*, will he? Well, well, that will be the day when there is fishing at the *cairidh*, and us stuck with a factor that would grudge losing a single scale off a salmon.'

The stranger had fairly got old Seumas going, and we had to hear all his tales of the great fishings there had been when he was a boy; how, when the signal was given by Mairi Beathag's father that the tide had fallen far enough for a start to be made, the men would wade out to the *cairidh* with their landing nets — those of them short in the leg sometimes up to their neck in the water — and bring the fish to the shore, the catch divided between every house in the township, according to the size of the family.

I believe he would have gone on all night, old Seumas, if Rob had not fallen asleep where he sat. As I ran home, the hill looming black above the road against the night sky, I wondered if the stranger and Runag the monkey were sleeping sound on their bed of heather in the cave. There was a light showing in Mairi Beathag's house, but Mairi always had a lamp burning till all hours. They said she never went to bed at all, that she sat up every night waiting for her brother Ruairidh to come home, his supper set ready on the table, and himself drowned fishing lobsters all of forty years ago. But it was Mairi who had fed the stranger, whereas those who made mock of her would have been quick to bar the door on that dark man and his monkey.

I heard Fearghus Mor's voice booming out before I set foot inside the house, but I did not know what to say when I found the kitchen crowded with men, the fathers of Alasdair Ruadh, Niall, Tormod Beag, Aonghas and Seoras all there.

'Did you hear the news, Calum Og?' the *cailleach* said, quick to take advantage of the silence that fell at the opening of the door, adding, before I could speak, 'The factor is hurt bad, lying senseless, poor man. I knew fine he would come to grief galloping about the place on that black stallion of his, and the beast half wild.'

'I was there,' Fearghus Mor reminded her, his red face seeming to swell as he spoke, he was that puffed up with his own importance, 'standing right by the door o' the stables when the factor was thrown — the only one to see it happen — and I am telling you the stallion was walking quiet as a lamb. Galloping! Good grief, what way could the beast gallop, and him just after having his last feed? — that full o' food and water he was not wanting to leave his stall. The pony was settled down for the night when the factor took the notion to ride out and see the coal boat make off, and he is not the man to be hard on the beast. Amn't I after telling you the factor was walking his pony just. Something must ha' stung the beast, he reared that sudden.'

'You would think the doctor would know what is wrong wi' him,' Alasdair Ruadh's father said. 'They say he is a great hand at mending broken bones and the like.'

'The factor's bones are not broken,' Fearghus Mor said. 'There is not a mark on the man, not a mark — and what way can the doctor see inside of him? When I saw him stretched out on the grass, not moving a whisker — and himself not falling heavy — I could not make it out. It was myself helped carry him into the Lodge, and when we laid him down on his bed he was breathing that slow and steady you would have sworn he was sleeping sound.'

'A pity he ever took the notion to ride out,' Tomas Caogach said, 'and the Lodge facing the sea, and himself with a great view o' the schooner supposing he never stirred from his hearth.'

'He must have hit his head bad,' Niall's father said.

'When the beast reared, he took a tumble on his shoulder,' Fearghus Mor declared. 'He did not strike his head.'

'But he has lost his senses, Fearghus,' Tomas Caogach said.

'Not able to say a word,' the *cailleach* added.

Their voices beat about my ears, but I was not hearing them. It was the deep slow voice of the stranger I was hearing, as he levelled his dark eyes at the shoemaker, and said '*But what if the factor does not say a word?*' — that was what I was hearing, that and the monkey's sudden sharp screech of terror at the blast on the silver whistle that had made no sound.

Every morning the doctor's gig bowled down the road and turned into the drive leading to the Lodge, and before the sun had reached his zenith the news that there was no change in the condition of the factor had spread to everyone in the township. At the end of the first week, the doctor took home a medical man from Edinburgh — a big man, they said, one who had tended the Queen when she was sick — and after he had gone the doctor's gig was seen only every second day. The word was that the big man from the city was without a cure; all he could say was that the factor was too poorly to be moved, and must be watched steady for the least sign of a change. Two nurses took up quarters in the Lodge, and were on the go day and night beside the factor's bed. But he never stirred, or uttered a single word, breathing slow and deep as he had done from the first — like a man in a trance, one of the nurses told Marsali.

The doctor came and went, and his visits got to be such a regular happening that nobody bothered to watch for the coming and going of his gig any more. Indeed, with September well broached, and the clear blue of the sky unbroken, not the least sign of an end to the sun, they were too taken up by the thought that their crops had been saved to pay any heed to what was going on at the Lodge.

Day after day, week after week, the sun shone. There had never been such a blaze of colour in the place; the deep blue of the loch vying with that of the sky; the heather purpling the hills and the bracken flaming bright. Between the turf dykes, on the narrow strips of arable running down to the shore, the crops prospered as never before. The sickly shaws of the potatoes sprouted strong and green, and the burgeoning corn thickened fast, growing tall and heavy under the hot sun. The men took their reaping hooks down from the rafters and made ready for the harvest, close grouped together by the dyke at the bottom of Tomas Caogach's croft, honing the blades to a fine edge on their stones when they were not busy with talk, that quick to laugh you would have thought they had taken strong drink. It was the sun that had made them drunk. Even the sternest of them seemed to be softened by the sight of the harvest coming good, and all of us boys were allowed to go our own way. Indeed, the sight of us wading out into the loch at the behest of the stranger seemed to make them laugh the more.

Every day, according to the state of the tide, we gathered on the shore in answer to the shrill notes of the stranger's whistle. In the beginning, he had us search the tideline beyond the headland for driftwood, and he made hand-barrows from the wood we brought back — made them so good that Uilleam Dubh, whose trade it was, swore that he must have worked as a carpenter. At the ebb tides, we waded out to sea behind him, and he loaded our barrows with stones from the ruined *cairidh*. We carted the stones ashore, the shafts of the barrows borne on our shoulders, and dumped them above the high-water mark, and rid them of the clinging weed.

Once all the stones had been lifted, and assembled according to size — Fearghus Mor wanting to know was it a pyramid the Egyptian was raising — the building of the *cairidh* began. The stranger set the stones in place as we carted them out to him on the handbarrows, starting at the Lodge end of the trap, and slowly working out in the same sweeping horseshoe curve that the old wall had taken. He was a good worker, quick at the job without ever seeming to hurry, and he had a great eye for selecting the right stone straight off. Indeed, he was a better hand at drystone walling below water than many a one I have seen at the work on dry land. When I asked him where he had learned the knack all he would say was that there was always a place for the right shaped stone, and you had to build that way, not taking the first stone that came to hand and trying to make it fit — that would put the wall out of true, and it would not endure. Seoras the dummy, who never took his eyes off him, was quick to grasp the knack. Before a week was past the stranger had Seoras working alongside him at the building, while the rest of us carted stones out to them.

Nobody wearied at the building of the *cairidh*, there were that many willing hands on the go. Even Eachann Crubach laboured down to the shore on his crutches every day, just to be along with us. There was not much that Eachann Crubach could do seeing he had been born with useless twisted sticks of legs that would not have supported a bairn — and himself sixteen, and as heavy built across the shoulders and chest as a grown man. But he sat himself down on the big flat rock that Runag the monkey had selected as his throne, keeping the beast company and the rest of us cheery with his chaff. Eachann's tongue was never still, and before the stranger was done with him his hands were not idle either.

One morning we found Runag scrambling up and down a load of long ash saplings that were propped against the big flat rock. Seoras the dummy grew another six inches straight off when the stranger signed to him to get on with the building of the wall of the *cairidh* by himself. He stayed with Eachann Crubach, the two of them working together, the stranger showing Eachann how to make a landing net frame from a sapling. It was easy done; the sapling bent into a long U-shape, the gap between the sides bridged by a cross-bar about a third of the way in from the ends, and the open ends brought together in a blunt point, and bound with twine. When they had made a stack of frames, Eachann Crubach was left on his own with a whalebone needle and thread, busy making bag nets for the frames, a job that did not hinder his tongue any.

It was Eachann who was the first to see the factor's coach draw up at the porch of the Lodge. 'If that is the Queen come to open the *cairidh*,' he called to me, as a dumpy figure in black climbed down slowly from the carriage, 'we had best send word we are not ready.'

The stout woman waited at the step, and I watched as a girl got out. The two of them went into the house together; the governess leading the way, Lady Elizabeth at her back.

Marsali came up to the house at dusk that night, but she was wise enough not to give me her message until we were on our own, and I was walking her back to the Lodge. Not that she came straight out with it; she was too wild with me for that, although to look at her you would not have known she was the least troubled.

She waited until we had reached the gate by the sea wall — the servants being forbidden to use the drive — and stood with her back to it, looking out across the loch. 'It is a beauty of a night,' she said, gazing up at the fat harvest moon and the winking stars. And then, barely pausing to draw breath, knowing fine I was not prepared for what she had coming, 'Lady Elizabeth is wanting to see you.'

'Me?' I said, quaking inside, as I digested the name. 'Why should the laird's cousin be wanting to see me?'

'You should know,' Marsali said.

'Me?'

'Aye, you,' she said sharply.

'What did she say?'

'She said she wanted a message taken to a boy called Calum-something, who lived on the other side of the bay from the old wreck, and I would — .'

'How do you know it was me she wanted? There are plenty other Calums in the place.'

'Not with a mop of hair the colour o' bleached straw.'

'She never said that.'

'She did.'

'Never.'

'She did so. She has it all writ down.'

'What are you on about, girl?'

'Lady Elizabeth keeps a journal.'

'What is a journal?' I said, that desperate to know I had to let on I was ignorant.

'A book o' happenings. She writes down where she has been every day, folk she has met — that kind o' thing.'

'How do you know?'

'She told me.'

'When?'

'Never you mind.'

'When she was down on her knees scrubbing the floor o' the kitchen along wi' you,' I said, fairly spitting the words out at her, 'is that when she told you?'

'She tells me many a thing,' Marsali said, that cold and haughty I knew she was stung.

'She would, seeing the two o' you are such great friends,' I mocked. 'Lady Elizabeth, the laird's cousin, and Lady Marsali, the kitchen maid, queen o' the dirty pots.'

She hit me such a stinger across the face with her open hand that the tears sprang to my eyes. I seized her wrist, and we stood there, glaring at each other. There were tears in her eyes, too.

'Let go o' my wrist,' she said, her voice low but fierce.

I let go of her wrist, but neither of us made a move. The big moon hung low in the sky. I could hear the harsh cry of a corncrake's call coming from the tacksman's field, the bird keeping on as if his life depended on it. The tide washed the shore, steady as a heart-beat.

It was the longest silence that had ever come between Marsali and me. I swallowed. 'Did you tell her I was your brother?'

She nodded.

'It could mean trouble for you.'

'How?'

'Things I said to her.'

'You never let on to me that you had talked with her.'

'It was the night the girl first came here. How was I to know who she was?'

'You could have told me when you found out. I always told you things.'

'It was too late then. Besides, I felt a right clown.'

'What did you tell her?'

'How we were cleared from the glen to make room for the factor's brother and his sheep.'

'She never said a word o' that to me.'

'Maybe she is saving it for the factor.'

'He cannot hear, poor man.'

'Supposing he gets better?'

'She is away home to England the day after tomorrow.'

'The laird, then.'

'She says the laird is in India.'

'Were you having me on, Marsali, about her keeping that journal thing?'

'No fear.'

'And she has me in it?'

'For sure.' She put on a fancy English voice, her top lip rigid, even her bottom lip barely moving. 'Met strange boy by the beautiful old wreck. His feet needed washing.' She broke off, giggling. I could not stop laughing myself. 'Shhh!' she hissed. 'If the housekeeper hears, there will be murder. Right enough, you will be in her journal, but she says it is a secret. She has nobody to talk to; it is all old folk about her at her father's house, and that governess woman along wi' her wherever she goes.'

'Has she not got brothers and sisters?'

'No, she is the only one.'

'She must ha' said why she wants to see me.'

'No, she did not. Look, Calum Og, I must away.'

She opened the gate, and slipped inside. 'Marsali,' I hissed, as she turned to go, 'where am I to see the girl?'

'At the fish weir on the river,' she said. 'Tomorrow, at mid-day.'

'Will the old wife be along wi' her?'

'Who?'

'The governess woman.'

'Pity you, boy,' Marsali giggled, 'if she is.'

I could still hear her giggling to herself, as she scampered off along the path to the back of the Lodge.

I saw her through a tracery of branches, the sun gleaming on the silver birch boughs, thick with leaves that were turning pale gold. She was sitting on the weir, her back to me, looking up to the glen. Her hair was lighter than I had thought, near enough the colour of the birch leaves. There was no sign of the stout woman in black, but I cast a sharp eye about as I moved through the trees along the path by the river bank.

'You were wanting to see me,' I said to her back.

She gave a little cry, getting to her feet, and swinging round in the one movement, her hair a flurry of bright gold. 'I didn't hear you,' she said, her eyes dropping — as I knew they would — to my bare feet. Those who are never free of boots expect everyone to make as much clatter as an iron-shod horse.

'Do you remember the talk we had down on the shore?' she said.

I nodded.

'You didn't know who I was, did you?'

I shook my head.

She gave a little nervous laugh. 'It was wrong of me. I should have told you — told you who I was.'

She looked the same to me as the girl I had first seen that night in July when I had got up from the old wreck and stood before her; she had the same open, eager face, the same lack of guile in the wide eyes that looked straight into mine. She had not changed. But there was a difference, right enough, in knowing her name, knowing the title that went along with that name, knowing her to be the cousin of the laird. She could stay the same, but I could not. She had her place, and I had mine — and in my place you kept a still tongue in your head, if you were wise.

'Well, I've thought a great deal about what you said,' she went on, 'about your father having the thatch torn from his house, and being forced away from his croft, and I have tried to find out more about it.' My face must have betrayed me, because she said quickly, 'Oh, I didn't say a word to Captain Elliot,' — and it was queer hearing the factor given his name; to us he was just 'the factor', like the one before him, and the one that would take his place through time — 'I am not so silly, the Captain might not have understood, although it's not quite fair to say that, when he is so beastly ill. But I did try to find out what had really happened from other — other people when I was staying with them.' She gave her little nervous laugh. 'Because you were not born, you see, when all these changes took place. I mean, you only know what you were *told* by other people — other crofters.'

I nodded.

'The changes were all for the people's own good really,' she said. 'You see, there were far too many people, and not enough land, and to make the land pay you must have lots and lots of sheep, not heaps of little crofts, each crofter trying to keep a few cows and a tiny flock of sheep. If the people had been left like that they would have become poorer and poorer as there were more and more of them. So the proprietors had to make it easier for them to make a better living. Some proprietors went to great expense, and purchased a passage to the colonies for their tenants.'

Like the men of Lorgill, I thought; Lorgill, the glen of the deer's cry. The sheriff officer and four policemen had come to Lorgill of a summer's afternoon, and the people were told a ship awaited them in Loch Snizort, bound for Nova Scotia; and they had to take the long march over the moor to the loch, on pain of the jail, all save the old and infirm among them, who were put to the County Poorhouse. The old men spoke of it still, and it near fifty years since Lorgill was cleared.

The laird had not gone to that expense for us.

'We were put to the shore,' I said.

'That was to enable you to earn a better living from the sea,' she said, 'and not have to depend entirely upon the land. I was told by — well, by a gentleman who knows about these things, that once you have managed to build boats and things, it will be a very prosperous life for you here.'

It was in me to say that we were not fisher folk, that we were ignorant of the ways of the sea, that it was only the wanderers and the desperate among us who became seafarers and fishers, that it was the land we knew best and the raising of crops and cattle — but I held my tongue.

'You do see, don't you?' she said, frowning, she was that anxious for me to understand. 'I didn't want to leave for home without seeing you, and have you think I was not the least bit interested in what you had to say. But my papa says there is always more than one side to a story, and I wanted you to know what really happened. You do see that?'

I nodded, but words rose strong within me, words that could

not be contained, no matter what. 'But my father,' I said, 'he had the thatch torn from his roof, that was right enough. I was not telling lies. That was not a made-up story. My father had the thatch torn from his roof. My mother was there that day. She was put from the house, and in freezing cold, ice on the river.'

'I didn't forget,' she said, fairly bubbling over in her eagerness to explain it to me. 'When I was at Dunvegan, I asked Mr Forsyth, the lawyer, to tell me exactly what happened when a tenant was served with a notice of eviction, and Mr Forsyth told me that if the notice was not in order, or if the tenant had a just complaint against it, he could engage a lawyer, or go to the Court himself, and state his case before the Sheriff. It is what is known as an appeal. But, of course, if no appeal is lodged the eviction must take place, according to the law. Perhaps your father did not know that he had the right of appeal.'

I nodded, wondering what like it would be to have a governess trailing around the country at your elbow, teaching you special, no other scholars to worry about. You would learn all the words fast, and how to say them properly, and many a thing besides, but there was more to learning than that. What way could a poor man get a lawyer to speak up for him – even supposing the lawyer was willing – and himself without money to pay the lawyer's big fee? And who but a fool would get up in Court and whisper a word against the factor, and himself and the Sheriff old cronies, exchanging visits every week in life, and it well known that it took four men to carry the Sheriff to his coach after a night at the factor's claret. I did not blame the laird's cousin. She was not to know. The learning she got was different altogether from mine.

'You will miss Marsali,' she said.

'Miss her?' I stammered.

'When she leaves here, and enters service with us.'

I swallowed. 'When will that be?'

'Well, I will have to speak to my papa about Marsali, once I am home, but I am sure he will engage her. Your sister is a very bright girl, and a good worker. I should not be surprised if she became a lady's maid when she is older.'

'Is that good?'

'Marsali would say so.'

She sat down on the weir, scuffing at the ground with her toe of her boot, and it came to me that she did not know how to break off the talk, and her sitting was my signal to go. 'Well, I must away,' I said, itching to be gone, certain sure the stout woman in black would march down the path at any moment, but not knowing how to take my leave of her, until the words of Mata the tinker sprang unbidden to my tongue. 'A safe going,' I said.

'Thank you,' she said, giving a little nod of her head.

She was Lady Elizabeth and I was Marsali's brother, and neither of us any the better off for knowing that much more about the other, so far as I could see.

My head was buzzing with the thought that Marsali had never let on to me that she was making off. I had always known that she would leave the place one day, but I was certain sure that I would be the first to know what was in her mind, and the two of us would plan together how she would break the news of her going to the *cailleach* and Tomas Caogach. How could she even *think* of asking for a place at the house of the laird's cousin without ever letting on to me? What would she say if I blurted out the news to our mother? It would be the price of her if I did. The *cailleach* would take a fit.

I heard the thin, shrill notes of the stranger's whistle, calling that the tide was at the ebb, and the hurt was gone from me at the sound, the anger and the jealous spite washed clean away. It was as if the laird's cousin had never spoken Marsali's name. I ran for the shore, the only thought in my head the need to get there quick and share in the work of the *cairidh*.

14

It was good working at the building of the *cairidh*. There was talk and chaff on the go all the time, forever bubbling over into laughter. But good as it was to be working together as one, with no arguments or fights to spoil it on us, there was more to it than that. At first, it was in me to believe that the shrill music of the stranger's whistle — and the queer little tune he played to call us to the shore — had cast a spell upon us, banishing all strife. It was strange, right enough, the way the first high-pitched note was enough to set our feet moving, only the old ones taking no heed, wanting to know what was our hurry, seeming deaf to the summons. But that was no more than a foolish fancy. I knew fine it would take more than a tune played on a silver whistle to make the Marag take care where he dropped a heavy stone for fear it would crush a scuttling crab. And it came to me through time that it was the wonder of the strange new world we were seeing — a world that had been under our nose all the time, and ourselves blind to it — that had made the Marag spare the fleeing crab.

Working at the *cairidh* every day when the tide was at the ebb, we had become the close familiars of an underwater world where great forests of sea-ware — crimson and gold and green and purple — nodded with the pull of the tide, like trees bending before a breeze of wind; forests that teemed with living creatures. Sea-anemones clustered like flowers on the rocks; tiny jelly-fish, edged with spots, trailing long white fringes like finely woven shawls, drifted by; starfish galore glittered through the tangle; silver eels, no bigger than a man's little finger, darted in and out of the swaying fronds that were beaded black with tiny mussels, each moored to its anchorage by a silken cable; and crabs of all shapes and sizes, kept wary watch, sometimes leaving the shelter of their weed-covered rocks to scuttle across the sandy bottom.

Our work was governed by the tides, and it was as if something of the slow, strong pull of the sea had entered our being, making us aware that the pulse of life of all living creatures beat with our own. It came to me that we were not just building a fish trap. With every stone that went into the wall of the *cairidh*, we seemed to be weaving a web that bound us ever closer to the living world, and I had the notion that the sun would always sparkle on the loch, that winter would never come, so long as the work went on.

It was a Thursday morning, the tenth day of October by the count of the calendar, that the last stone was put in place. By my reckoning, it was the fiftieth day since the coming of the stranger, and the air as warm as the August morning he first came ashore from the coal boat, the sky and the loch as bright a blue, but the place looking different altogether now that the corn was cut, the sun golden on the stooks that abounded on every croft.

The stranger handed over the last stone to Seoras, and the dummy's face was a sight to behold as it dawned upon him that he was to get to lay the very last stone of all. It was a big square stone, straight-sided, flat at the bottom, curving a little at the top; the twin of a hundred others that had gone into the making of the top of the wall. But Seoras would know its face again, that was a sure thing, seeing the way he gazed upon it, and held it clutched tight to his chest, as if he had gained a treasure beyond price. The only sound was the strong wash of the incoming tide, and the cry of a lone gull circling overhead. Nobody spoke as he lowered it slowly into the gap in the top of the wall. The stone fitted that neat you would have thought it had been trimmed special for the job.

A great cheer went up, as it slid into place, Eachann Crubach joining in from his seat on Runag's stone, the monkey dancing up and down beside him. Seoras was the only one not hearing, gazing down at the stone he had set in place as if he could not believe what he saw.

'That is her done, boys,' the stranger said, casting his arm out in a wide sweep that took in the giant horse-shoe that was the wall of the *cairidh*. 'Let there be good fishing.'

A sudden babble of excited chatter broke out, everyone talking at once. We waded ashore, splashing one another with water, shouting and laughing fit to bring the *Ceistear* down on us, and his house far up the hill on the other side of the bay.

Eachann Crubach hoisted himself up on his crutches, and hastened down the shore to meet us, caught up in the excitement. 'When do we make a start?' he cried.

'We will give her a try after the second tide,' the stranger said, 'at the midday ebb tomorrow.'

They all clustered around him, wanting to know did he expect a good fishing. I was the only one watching Runag the monkey. The beast was standing on his hind legs on the flat rock he had

111

made his own, his arms raised on high, spread wide to the sun. He fairly had a notion for the sun, Runag. I felt the stranger's eyes on me. He gave a sharp whistle, and the monkey dropped down and bounded across the sand to him.

'Runag will bring us luck,' Eachann Crubach said. 'We will have a great fishing, I know it.'

The turf dyke at the bottom of the crofts was the boundary between the believers and the unbelievers, although, in truth, my own belief was ebbing as fast as the tide, seeing the stranger made no move to try the *cairidh*. He was sitting on the big flat rock, Runag the monkey on one side of him, Eachann Crubach on the other, the rest of us gathered around them. At our back, all the men of the township had come together at the bottom of Fearghus Mor's croft. They were leaning over the dyke, like spectators waiting to see a show at the horse fair. The whole crowd of them had come to get a good laugh, and Fearghus Mor was not the one to disappoint them.

'What is keeping you?' he bellowed. 'Is there such a haul o' herring in the *cairidh* you are needing us to come and lend a hand at the netting?'

That fairly had them rolling about laughing, but I heard old Seumas pipe up above the racket, 'The laugh will be on you, Fearghus, supposing the herring take the notion to come up the loch the way they did in the old days.'

'The herring are gone since years,' Fearghus Mor boomed. 'What use is a *cairidh* when the shoals stay clear o' the loch? As well for a man without horses to waste his time building stables.'

I wondered what was holding the stranger back as the stretch of beach widened before us, and the topmost stones of the wings of the *cairidh* started to break clear of the ebb tide. He sat there as if he had not a care in the world, heedless of the laughter behind him, tossing a bright coloured pebble from hand to hand, teasing Runag who was trying to snatch it from him. But it was as if he had read my thoughts, for he tossed the pebble to the monkey and rose to his feet. 'Well, Eachann,' he said, stretching lazily, 'we had best give one o' your landing nets a try.' He picked up a net, and strode down the beach, the rest of us hard at his heels, Eachann Crubach's crutches thudding down on the wet sand as he strained to keep up. I went back to the rock, and snatched up a net, and ran after them.

'Wait you, Calum Og,' he said, when he saw me with the big

112

landing net, 'you would be out o' your depth, boy.' He gave me his quick smile. 'Besides, it is better that they laugh at me supposing the *cairidh* is empty o' fish.'

We stood at the water's edge watching him wade out to the *cairidh*. The sea was up to his chest before he came to a stop. With his left hand over the blunt end of the frame, and his right hand gripping the cross-bar, he thrust the net deep down into the water.

What a laugh went up from the men at the dyke — a great roar of laughter, topped by a mocking cheer — when he raised the net out of the water, and the dripping bag hung slack, empty of fish, the ash frame trailing a long strand of weed.

'It is early days,' Eachann Crubach said, hunched over his crutches. 'Who would be looking for a catch at the very first fishing o' the *cairidh*?'

Eachann, for one, I thought. But nobody had the heart to remind him of his boasts. We were all too down in the mouth to utter a word.

The stranger shifted his stance, and thrust the net down again. I looked back at the heads and shoulders of the men leaning over the dyke, wishing that it would collapse and plunge them into the drain below. Not that it would have bothered them seeing the drain was dry after the long spell of fine weather. Runag the monkey was up on his hind legs, his arms raised to the sun. 'Let the monkey have a shot,' a voice shouted, and there was another burst of laughter.

'Look!' Rob cried, leaping up and down, arms threshing in his excitement.

The stranger was lifting the net terrible slow, and the reason was easy seen once it broke the water. The bag was heavy with fish, gleaming silver in the sun. He hefted the frame across his shoulder, and turned for the shore.

The sky was suddenly full of screaming gulls, swooping low over the *cairidh*, their noisy clamour filling the air. And the gulls were not the only ones to come quick. The men were scrambling on to the top of the dyke, and jumping over the drain. They ran down the shore to the big flat rock, the first of them snatching up the landing nets that were lying by the rock. Those at the front who had seized nets raised them on high, and they all gave a cheer, I will say that for them — and no mockery about it this time — as the stranger strode up the beach, and dumped his catch. I never saw a sight to equal that of the silvery herring tumbling out of his net. Seoras the dummy grabbed at the landing net I was holding, and went wading out, near falling over himself in his hurry to get to the *cairidh*.

'Good on you!' Fearghus Mor cried. He was beaming all over his big red face, and he clapped the stranger on the back, that friendly in his approach you would have thought he was one of us and not the leader of those who had made mock of the fishing. 'Right enough,' he went on, 'I had my doubts about the herring coming back, but I am not the one to take it on the nose seeing I was wrong for once. Not me. No, nor any o' the rest of us. You will not want for willing hands at the fishing o' the *cairidh*, you may be sure o' that.' He turned on the rest of us, as if we had been hindering him. 'You boys make off home for pails, and be quick about it. Tell the womenfolk to have their knives ready; there will be plenty gutting for them before we are done.'

He was a big blow, Fearghus Mor, bossing us about as if we had been as foolish as himself, and ourselves the ones who had worked with the stranger at the building of the *cairidh*, and made possible the fishing. He was in his glory ordering folk about, and he was still busy at it when we got back with the pails, telling men where to dump their catch, and getting us to lay out a line of marker stones, one for each house in the township, to mark the shares when it came to the division of the catch. There was a steady passage of men from the *cairidh* to the shore with loaded nets, others wading out again to try for more. When the last net was emptied old Seumas had the nerve to make out that it was not much of a fishing, nothing like the landings that had been made in the old days, although he allowed that we might do better on the second day. It is great how old men do not like to be beat, always making out that nothing can compare to the great days of their youth. But I had never seen the like of it, that was a sure thing. And no matter what the shoemaker said, it took Fearghus Mor and Tomas Caogach long enough to divide the catch between the marker stones.

Fearghus Mor straightened his back, and looked around. 'Where is he?' he said, wiping his hands on his trousers.

That was when we noticed that the stranger had gone. In all the excitement of the fishing, nobody had seen him make off.

'Well, well, he is a queer fellow, the Egyptian,' Fearghus Mor said. 'What came over him at all, not waiting for his share? Murchadh,' he said to the Marag, 'away and take Mairi Beathag her herring; the stranger's share is in along wi' her own.'

'You forgot the monkey, Fearghus,' Seumas said solemnly. 'What about his share?'

'That will be the day,' Fearghus Mor boomed, too stupid to see the joke, 'I would as soon give our herring away to a pack o' tinkers as see good food wasted on the like o' that beast.'

Niall was the first to spot their coming, although it was the cattle he was supposed to be looking for. The three of us — Niall and Tormod Beag and me — had gone to gather the township's cattle, and herd them home from the common grazing, but we had dallied on a level stretch of green to try our strength at putting the stone, and now that the sun was down we were impatient to find the beasts.

Not that it was near dark. Dusk was only just starting to fall, and the colours of the moor seemed to glow the brighter with the sun gone; the green of the mosses mingling with the brown of the peat hags and the purple of the heather and the russet of the bracken. Even the outcrops of bare rock had acquired a warm hue in the weeks of hot sun, not looking like rocks at all, but bright islands set in a many coloured sea.

Niall had run on ahead of us, climbing a green hillock to scan the moor for the beasts. The grazing was that good the cattle were never in a hurry to come home these days, not like the weeks when the mist lay heavy on the hill and we would find them waiting at the dyke, eager for the byre. Tormod Beag said, 'Did you get a feed o' herring?'

'I had a great feed,' I said, and so I had, two whole herring all to myself, that tasty I very near ate my fingers when I was done.

'Come quick!' Niall called, beckoning to us.

We knew him too well to run. He was a great hand at jokes, Niall, but if he thought he could have us on that a beast was trapped in a bog he was mistaken. The moor was that dry you could walk where you pleased without even wetting the soles of your feet.

'Where are they?' Tormod Beag shouted.

'The cattle? Over by the burn.' He beckoned urgently again. 'It is not the cattle, you clowns. Come quick.'

That got us moving, and we ran to the hillock, and scrambled up to join him. He pointed east where the road wound over the moor to the high pass. 'See?'

'See what?' I said.

'Whereabouts?' Tormod Beag wanted to know.

'Have you not eyes the pair o' you?' Niall cried. 'Where the road comes round the shoulder o' hill. Follow the dust cloud.'

They were easy seen once you knew where to look; a long, long straggling line of carts, piled high with gear, some of them with young ponies walking at the back, tethered to the tailboards; men and women and children plodding along at the side of the carts — the long, long procession making its slow way towards us.

'Tinkers!' Tormod Beag exclaimed.

'They have some nerve,' Niall said. 'I never thought they would ever show face again.'

'Maybe they are just passing through,' I said.

'And it dark soon?' Niall said. 'They are making for their old camping ground, that is a sure thing.' He pointed across to the burn. 'There are the cattle. We had best make over and get them moving.'

We had herded the cattle off the road, and on to the path leading down to our township, when a wild stirk belonging to Tormod Beag's father doubled back the way and made off up the road. Tormod Beag scrambled up the bank to try to head him off, but the beast was too fast for him. He had a long chase up the road before he managed to get in front of the stirk and head him off. When he brought the stirk back, instead of going the long way round to the start of the path, he drove the beast down the steepest part of the bank. Many a goat would have come to grief on that steep slope, but the wild stirk slithered down without breaking a leg, and trotted off after the rest of the cattle. Indeed, it was Tormod Beag we thought had hurt himself when he stayed near the top of the bank, bent double.

'That beast must ha' given him a knock,' Niall said, and the two of us scrambled up the bank towards him.

As we drew near, Tormod Beag put a finger to his lips. 'It is the stranger,' he said softly. 'I reckon he is making off.'

He led the way to the top of the bank, keeping low, and pointed to the sheep track that criss-crossed its way up the face of the hill to the moor. The stranger was toiling up the track, a black figure against the hill, Runag the monkey perched on his shoulder, his sailcloth pack slung on his back. We watched him until he was out of sight. He never once looked back.

'That is him away,' Tormod Beag said. 'I wondered why he made off from the fishing wi' never a word.'

'It is queer him making off like that,' I said, 'seeing the time he has stayed with us working on the *cairidh*, and himself the one that was right about the herring coming back.'

'Aye, but it was easy seen he was not pleased at the way Fearghus Mor took over and started ordering folk around like he was the big man,' Tormod said.

'But it is a queer time to be crossing the moor wi' the night coming on.'

'It will be dark before he is anywhere near the pass,' Tormod Beag agreed. 'I would not fancy it supposing I had a lion to guard me, and not just a wee monkey. Where can he be going?'

'I know where he is off to,' Niall declared.

We looked at him, but he kept his mouth shut until the pair of us were forced to say, 'Where?'

'To see his friends, the tinkers.'

'How do you know they are friends o' his?' I said.

'Well, he is one o' themselves.'

'Not him.'

'He is maybe not a right tinker,' Niall allowed, 'but he is a man that travels the road, so he is near enough one o' themselves.'

'Niall has got it,' Tormod Beag said. 'The stranger would never be making for the moor, and it dark soon, unless to call on the tinkers.'

There was no answer to that, and I was in bed, near sleeping, when it came to me that either the two of them were wrong, or the stranger was not as other men. I wondered how I could have been so slow not to tumble to it right off. We three had been the only ones on the high moor, and we were using our eyes searching for the cattle, but even then we had not spotted the approach of the tinkers' carts until we climbed the hillock. It would have been different if they had already reached their camp, and the smoke of their fires had signalled their presence far and wide.

In my mind's eye I saw that slow caravan of carts crossing the empty moor, and the dark figure of the stranger against the hill, toiling slow up the sheep track with the monkey on his shoulder. By the time he reached their camp by the burn below Reieval, they would be setting up their tents, lighting their fires, the women bringing out the cooking pots to prepare food. He could not have timed it better if he had known. But *how* could he have known, when Niall, Tormod Beag and me were the only ones in all our township to have seen the coming of the tinkers?

15

The tide had not long been on the turn — a thin crescent of wet rocks on the foreshore the only sign that the ebb was under way — but the shore was thick with people gathered for the second fishing of the *cairidh*. This time there was no line of grinning faces standing behind the turf dyke at the bottom of the crofts; the men were sitting on the rocks close at our backs, as eager as ourselves to see a start made. Near everyone in the place that was able was gathered on the shore, except the *Ceistear* and Mr Ferguson. The *Ceistear* was away in Raasay, attending the burial of his sister, who had been married to a man from that island, and the Head Keeper had gone to Glenelg — trying for a new job with a big laird on the mainland, according to Fearghus Mor. But Gilleasbuig, the ground officer, was still with us, busy threading his way through the crowd, all smiles and quick nods and whispered words, big ears on the flap steady, pale blue eyes prowling swift from face to face, eyes that could pry an inventory out of a person quicker than the pen of a clerk. I saw his eyes light on the thin, white face of Coinneach Beag, sitting with his back against the ruins of the old kelp-burners' hut where he was shielded from the sun, and flit to the lined, weathered face of Coinneach's father, Dughall. The ground officer would be wondering if Dughall had used the money put by for the year's rent — and the Rent Collection due next month — to pay the doctor for attending his crippled son.

He was as frail as a dry leaf, poor Coinneach; the least puff of wind, it seemed to me, would be enough to blow him over. Coinneach Beag had been smitten with the fever the year of the long drought. He had never risen from his bed from that day to this, and there had been three Rent Collections since that dry Spring. His father had carried him down to the shore wrapped in a plaid, and he sat rigid, his useless legs sticking out as stiff as boards. Coinneach was ages with Marsali, but he looked that small wrapped in the big plaid, it was as if he had not grown at all since he was stricken with the fever. The *cailleachs* were making a fuss of him, but they would be the very ones to turn on Dughall if the boy took a bad turn after his outing to the shore.

All the old wives had come down to watch, that sure there would be fish to carry home not a single one of them was without a pail or an empty meal bag. They sat in chattering groups on the grassy mounds above the rocks; the girls, all of a giggle, drifting in clinging coveys between the womenfolk and us boys. We had been the first to make for the shore, and had taken up our stance around the big flat rock that Runag the monkey had made his own. But Runag was not there, nor the stranger. Eachann Crubach and Seoras the dummy, sitting side by side, had the rock to themselves, the still centre of a rage of talk about the stranger. They all had their own idea why he had left us without a word — and they were not slow in speaking up — but Eachann Crubach was as deaf to the talk as the dummy, his gloomy gaze fixed on the retreating tide, that down in the mouth his quick tongue was still for once.

What with all the talk on the go, and every eye latched fast on the loch to measure the fall of the tide, not a one of us was aware of his coming, until we heard that slow, deep voice at our back, saying, 'Well, boys, is it to be a good fishing?'

He was standing behind the big flat rock, the monkey perched on his left shoulder, smiling at us as he had done that day in August when we first met. He laid his hands on the shoulders of Eachann and Seoras; strong hands, broad and square, white scars against the brown skin where they had suffered bad knocks; the hands of a worker. Runag the monkey dropped down on to the rock, his sharp, pointed little face looking from Seoras to Eachann as if he could not understand why they were not making a fuss of him. But the pair of them had eyes only for the stranger.

Eachann Crubach was the first to get his tongue working, and himself the one to have been more cast down than any of us. 'We were after thinking you had left us,' he said.

'Without a word?' the stranger smiled. 'I am not the one to make off without a word to my friends.'

'You went off yesterday without a word,' Eachann mumbled. 'I made up to the cave after dark, and you were gone. I was thinking you were away for good.'

He had never let on to us that he had gone to the cave, Eachann Crubach, and himself a cripple on crutches. It was a wonder to me how he had managed such a climb.

'You were not needing me yesterday,' the stranger said. 'You got the fish netted no bother.' He lifted his hand and brought it down again on Eachann's shoulder. 'But I am back along wi' you today for a last word before I take the road.'

'Why must you go?' Eachann Crubach said, scowling down at his crutches.

The stranger smiled his quick smile. 'I have my road to travel,' he said, 'and you — .' That was as far as he got. Fearghus Mor's big hand came slapping down on his back, cutting the words off short. 'Well, friend,' he boomed, 'it is myself well pleased to see you. Did you get your share o' the catch? I had it sent up special along wi' Mairi Beathag's.'

'Mairi was well pleased,' the stranger said.

'And there will be more for you today,' Fearghus Mor went on, pointing to the gulls wheeling and crying over the *cairidh*, 'or there would not be that racket going on out there.' He cast a quick glance over his shoulder, and I could have sworn it was directed at Gilleasbuig. The ground oficer was standing by the ruins of the kelp-burners' hut, his back to us, an ear cocked close to Tomas Caogach, who was laying off his chest to him. 'What do you say to starting off the fishing for us?'

'You are not needing me to show you how to fish the *cairidh*,' the stranger said.

Fearghus Mor shot another quick glance over his shoulder. 'Aye, but it is yourself that has the luck,' he said, thrusting a landing net into the stranger's hands. 'That is the way of it at the fishing; the one wi' the luck must always make the first shot.'

That was true enough. I had often heard old Seumas say that one man, known for his luck with the herring, had always led the fishing of the *cairidh* in the old days. But there was more to it than that with Fearghus Mor. The big fellow was fly enough to know that the factor might get better, or another take his place, and if ever there came a day of reckoning, and the ground officer was summoned to report to the factor, they would be able to make out that it was the stranger who had led the fishing of the *cairidh*, and put the blame on him.

The crowd closed in at our back, even the women coming forward, as the stranger walked down to the sea, the landing net over his shoulder, followed by Fearghus Mor. The two of them waded out to the *cairidh*, Fearghus Mor well to the rear. The tide was not so far out as it had been when the stranger made a start the day before and the water was up to his shoulders before he came to a stop. Every eye was on him, as he raised a hand to break the glare of the sun on the water, and peered into the depths. He beckoned to Fearghus Mor, and the big fellow hurried to his side. They had their heads close together, and it was Fearghus Mor who made the first move. He turned for the shore, arms held high, breasting through the water at a stumbling run. He came splashing up the beach, as the stranger shifted his stance and forced the landing net down into the water.

'The *cairidh* —' Fearghus Mor shouted, his voice cracking in his excitement. He cleared his throat, and spat, and raised a dripping arm to wipe the sweat from his gleaming red face. 'The *cairidh* is a solid lump o' fish,' he cried. 'Herring galore! You never saw the like. Enough herring to last us the winter through, even supposing there was not another bite o' food in the place.' He stopped to draw breath. 'What a harvest!' he gloated, his eyes fairly popping. 'More than enough for every family in the place, and plenty left over for to sell. The factor will have a good Rent Collection this year, I am telling you. There is not a one need be a penny behind wi' the rent, and everyone able to do himself justice, secure against the winter wi' a full belly on him come what may.'

The stranger came up behind Fearghus Mor, the landing net bulging with fish, his back bowed against the weight. He swung the frame down from his shoulder, the herring pouring out, a stream of bright silver in the sun. 'You will be weary o' lifting herring,' he said, smiling his quick smile, 'before this day is done.'

Fearghus Mor was not hearing him. He strode forward and seized Tormod Gobha by the arm, tugged at the coat of Uilleam Dubh as the carpenter reached for a landing net, and jabbed a broad finger at Tomas Caogach, all the time barking his orders.

In all the days of my life I had never seen such a sight; the whole township congregated on the shore, working as one, men and women, young and old, everyone who was able on the go steady. Uilleam Dubh, the carpenter, fetched boards, and we raised mounds of stones to support the boards, so that the women had benches where they could work at gutting the herring as they were landed. Tormod Gobha made off to his smithy to get a horse harnessed to his big cart, and Tomas Caogach hurried away at the head of a party of women, out to lay hands on every empty barrel in the township, ready for Tormod Gobha to uplift. When the smith's cart reached the shore it was piled high with herring barrels, and bags of rock salt that the merchant had let them have on the strength of the catch. Others cut hazel saplings from the thicket by the burn at the bottom of Dughall's croft, and Uilleam Dubh fashioned the saplings into frames, while Eachann

121

Crubach, and five old women who had not been at the job since years, made nets.

It was some sight, I am telling you, a double line of men — Gilleasbuig, the ground officer, one of them, as much caught up in the excitement of the catch as the rest — moving slow but sure to and from the *cairidh*, the incoming line returning laden with bulging nets to add to the growing stack of herring piled on the beach. All of us boys, helped by the girls, shovelling the fish into creels, and carrying the loaded creels up the shore to the work benches; the women busy gutting, tongues going near as fast as their knives, their bare arms, from wrist to elbow, glittering bright with clinging fish scales; the old men and old women packing the gutted fish into the herring barrels, that neat and quick in their movements it was great to see them at work, the fish going in head to tail, packed in tight layers between layers of salt. Fires flaming, and the women brewing tea, but nobody stopping for a bite to eat, everyone set on clearing the *cairidh* of fish before the tide turned and came flooding back — and enough herring landed already to keep every pair of hands on the go for as long as there was light in the sky.

If the factor had risen from his bed and ridden down on us, mounted on his proud black stallion, not even the faint-hearted would have taken a blind bit of notice. There was such a bustle of work on the go, such an air of quick excitement — the clamour of the gulls barking overhead enough to deafen you — everyone knowing they had in their hands the means of deliverance from the worst the winter could do, that all fear of the factor had gone from them. Nobody so much as lifted his head to glance across at the Lodge, not even Gilleasbuig, the ground officer, and himself the one who would never be found on the side of the weak.

It was when I stopped work to take a quick drink of tea — and there is nothing so good as hot tea when you are dry with the sun and the brine is strong on your lips — that I noticed the stranger was missing. There was no sign of him anywhere. The crofts were bare of people, the corn stooks golden in the sun, Dughall the only living soul to be seen, moving slowly as he carried Coinneach Beag back to his bed.

Fearghus Mor stumped up the beach, and dumped his catch. 'The stranger is away,' I said.

The big fellow grunted. 'He will be back,' he said, tossing the words over his shoulder as he hastened out to the *cairidh*, 'looking for easy pickings like all the rest of his kind.'

The sun was a flaming red, low in the sky, when he came back. The *cairidh* had been cleared of fish, and two great stacks of herring were piled high on the beach, the flooding tide spurring us on as we shovelled the fish into Tomas Caogach's cart. It was the Sabbath in the morning, but the herring would keep well enough until Monday when we could finish the job of gutting and salting. Further up the beach, the full barrels were being rolled on to Tormod Gobha's cart, along with the work benches and landing nets and the rest of the gear. The women and the girls had gone home. Only the men and ourselves were left.

It was the Marag who saw them first, and no wonder seeing he was not keen on bending his back, forever leaning on his spade and pretending that something in the distance had caught his eye. He let out a shrill cry that brought everyone's head up, and we all followed his pointing finger. A long, straggling column, three and four abreast, was trailing down Mairi Beathag's croft to the shore; a ragged tribe of men and women, four score at the least count, near every single one of them carrying an old iron cooking pot or a tin pail, a few with creels slung over their shoulders. In the lead, a good ten paces ahead, strode the stranger, Runag the monkey perched on his shoulder.

He sprang on to the dyke at the foot of Mairi Beathag's croft, and stood there, looking out to sea, the rays of the setting sun casting a flame of light about his dark face. Standing there on top of the dyke, he seemed to me a giant, towering above us all. But that was a trick of the light. When he leapt down across the drain — the monkey clinging to his neck — he was reduced to his true stature.

It was the sight of the ragged tribe swarming over the dyke — score upon score of them — that jerked Fearghus Mor out of his trance. 'Tinkers!' he growled. 'The Egyptian is back wi' a tribe o' hungry tinkers at his heels, enough o' them to strip the shore bare o' herring quicker than a plague o' locusts could clear a field o' corn.' He started forward, the men surging along at his back.

The tinkers had stopped at the far side of the big flat rock. The stranger was speaking soft to them, holding them back by the look of it, the way he had his arms spread wide. Runag the monkey jumped off his shoulder, and bounded across to the rock, sitting cross-legged on his throne, peering around like a little old man in search of company.

Fearghus Mor came to a halt on the other side of the rock, the men standing shoulder to shoulder, close grouped at his back, barring the way to the herring stacks and Tomas Caogach's cart. It was like the games we played when we were little: the rock, a castle; rival armies lined up to do battle on either side of the fortress. But we had always played fair, careful to have the same number on either side, whereas the tinkers far outnumbered us. I had never seen such a crowd of them together at the one time. It was always in pairs, or at the most a group of three or four, that they appeared in our township. Seeing all those thin, dark faces assembled before us, it was like facing a hostile army from over the seas.

'What is that crew wanting?' Fearghus Mor shouted, as the stranger turned to face us.

The loose ends of the strip of gaudy calico that he wore at his neck fluttered in the breeze like a coloured banner. He showed his white teeth in an open smile, and said, as calm as you please, 'I have brought them down for herring.'

Fearghus Mor laughed. 'That will be the day when we give our herring away to a crowd o' thieving tinkers.'

'They are poor folk and hungry.'

'Then they should stop their thieving ways and work for an honest living like other folk.'

'They need food.' He pointed to the stacks of herring. 'You have plenty of herring there, more than enough for all of you.'

'You will get your share when we are done, and a count is made, but we are not for feeding our herring to that crowd o' wastrels. By the time they were done, there would not be fit leavings for a cat.'

'Are they to go without food?'

'They are not feeding on our herring,' Fearghus Mor said, 'I will tell you that, stranger.'

'Your herring?'

'Our herring. Fish that was won by the sweat of our brow, while that idle crew were lying about in their tents taking their ease.'

The stranger turned on his heel and went back to the tinkers. I could not hear what he was saying, but I saw the women and the old men among them moving to the back of the crowd, and the young ones forming up at the front. 'They are going to rush us,' Fearghus Mor muttered. 'Get stones at the back, and be ready to let fly.'

Behind the cover of the front rank, the men at the back snatched up stones from the shore. If the Marag tried to throw the monster of a rock he had picked up, I doubted if it would clear his father's head. It would be the price of the pair of them, if he felled Fearghus Mor.

The stranger started forward again, all but the women and the old men at his back. 'If you are not for giving,' he said, speaking loud for all to hear, 'I am for — .'

'Stone them!' Fearghus Mor shouted, ducking quick and seizing a rock himself.

'Wait!' I cried. But nobody heard me, and it would not have made a mite of difference if they had. They would have fought to hold the herring against redcoats with muskets, never mind a crowd of ragged tinkers, advancing slow behind the stranger.

A hail of stones flew over the head of the stranger, raining down on his followers, rattling against their pots and pails as they held them up to shield their heads. A lean, dark lad, not much older than myself by the look of him, fell to the ground. He was dragged away by two of his fellows. I saw him get to his feet, clutching his head, and stagger off after the fleeing women. A second shower of stones followed before the first was spent, and a third, the men laughing and shouting curses as they scrambled for more stones. The tinkers broke and fled, leaving the stranger standing there alone facing us, blood streaming down the left side of his face where a stone had gashed his cheek. The stranger and Runag. But the monkey was not facing us. Runag was lying where he had fallen, across the end of the big flat rock, long arms hanging down, one thin hand trailing in a shallow pool.

Nobody spoke. The wash of the tide was suddenly loud in my ears. The stranger moved across to the rock, walking stiff and slow. He lifted the monkey's head in his hands, and let it fall again. There was blood on his hands, blood that had not come from the cut on his cheek. He looked down at his hands, and his dark gaze raked the ring of silent men. He picked up the body of the monkey, cradling it close in his arms, and turned on his heel, striding out fast after the retreating tinkers. Nobody moved until they were all on the other side of the dyke; the broken host split into little groups drifting slow up Mairi Beathag's croft, like so much flotsam caught on an ebb tide.

'Well, that is them away, and good riddance to bad rubbish,' Fearghus Mor said. He picked up his spade. 'We had best get the herring loaded or the tide will be in on us.'

I was taking the short-cut home from the shore, climbing the dyke at the bottom of our croft, when Marsali called me. She rose from the shadow of a corn stook, and I trudged up the croft to her side. We sat down on the stubble, our backs against the stook. The full moon shone silver on the loch; the gables of the Lodge standing out sharp and clear. The front of the house was in darkness, not a light showing from within.

'I was up at the house,' she said. 'Tomas Caogach told me you had gone off on your own along the shore. The *cailleach* was getting worried.'

'I went out to the headland,' I said. 'I wanted off on my own after working along wi' the whole crowd o' them all day.'

'Were you not dead tired?'

I was that weary I did not know how I would rise again now that I had lain my bones to rest. 'No,' I said.

'You had a great fishing they tell me.'

'Aye, a great fishing.'

The stranger had said, '*If you are not for giving, I am for—*.' For what? For taking by force? But it was not a fighting army he had at his back. The first shower of stones had stopped them in their tracks; they had scattered at the second, and they were on the run before the third volley was in the air. And I had been every bit as stupid as the rest; I had thought he was holding the tinkers back when they first appeared, the way he had spoken to them with his arms spread wide. But the stranger's arms were always spread when he was talking, his hands forever reaching out as if he sought to pluck words from the air. What if he had only been going to say he was for taking his share of the fishing? He was entitled. He was the one who had shaped the building of the *cairidh*. Not even Fearghus Mor would have grudged him his share. But Fearghus Mor and the rest had not waited to find out. The sight of all those thin, dark, silent faces crowded at the stranger's back had driven them to attack. Right enough, the tinker tribe had a terrible fierce look. But Mata had *looked* fierce the day I first laid eyes on him; Mata who was a quiet man, once you got to know him, content so long as he had a fill for his pipe, and could wander free with his tribe.

Marsali said, 'I believe you are near sleeping.'

'Not me,' I said. 'You were saying we had a great fishing. So we did. If we eat all the herring we have put by, I doubt we will be growing scales before the winter is done.'

Marsali did not laugh; did not speak.

'What took you to the house at this time o' night?' I said.

. 'I had to take a message to the tacksman's wife,' she said, 'and the housekeeper told me I could go on home for a while.' She put a hand on mine. Her hand was cold. 'I got a scare.'

'What kind of a scare?'

'It was the factor. The sun was not long down, and the nurse on duty had not lit the lamps in his room. If you ask me, the nurse was dozing in her chair. Not that I blame her. What way could you stay awake with nothing to do but sit quiet in a chair, and himself never stirring, and it near dark in the room seeing the curtains were part drawn to keep out the sun.'

'The factor, girl,' I said. 'What about him?'

'He sat up in bed, shouting for his horse. The nurse near jumped out of her skin. She let out a shriek that could ha' been heard the other side o' the bay. Well, everyone in the house heard her, I am telling you. The housekeeper was down in the cellar, and she dropped a bottle o' claret. And the nurse went on shrieking. And the factor was roaring at her something terrible by this time.'

'Good grief, no wonder you got a scare.'

'It took the three o' them — the housekeeper and both o' the nurses to keep him in his bed.' She gripped my hand tight. 'He was not believing it was October. He kept on saying he must get down to the shore and see the coal boat make off.'

'He would not be remembering a thing since the night he got the knock on the head,' I said.

'The housekeeper sent the coachman off to fetch the factor's brother — the tacksman of Glenuig,' she rattled on. 'The tacksman said he must away to a proper hospital on the mainland. The factor was not for going, but the tacksman sorted him out. You never saw such a rush. A friend of the tacksman has a yacht in the harbour at Portree, and they are all away in the coach — the tacksman and the nurses and the factor. There is only me and the housekeeper kept on over the weekend. That is what I was wanting to see you about.'

'What?'

'The housekeeper always gets the Sabbath off. She makes over to her sister's at Cuil first thing, and she is never back until late at night. I am not fancying staying in the house on my own, and it the thirteenth tomorrow.'

She was terrible superstitious, Marsali; why, I knew not. Nothing bad had ever happened to her on the thirteenth.

'You could make an excuse to get out tomorrow night,' she

coaxed, 'and slip down to the Lodge. Will you do that for me, Calum Og?'

'If you have a good feed waiting.'

'I will have more than a feed for you.'

'What?'

'Some news.'

'What news?'

'A surprise.'

'I know it.'

'Not you.'

'I do.'

'Tell me, then.'

'You are away to work for the laird's cousin. If they do not catch you handing out great feeds to the stable boys, you might get to be a lady's maid.'

She was half crying, half laughing. 'How did you know?'

'Herself told me.'

'You never let on to me.'

'I was waiting for you to tell.'

'I got a letter today. Addressed to me, special, at the Lodge. Papers for to take me all the way from Strome to London. By the railway.'

'Are you not fear'd? Trains go at a terrible rate. Faster than the fastest coach. And great fires roaring in the engines — sparks flying all over the place — and making that much smoke you can see them miles off. Old Seumas has told me. He knows.'

'She has been on them herself,' Marsali said, hoisting her nose in the air, 'and she is younger than me, so why should I be fear'd?'

'You have a good nerve on you, girl. Have you told the *cailleach*?'

'Not yet.'

'When do you go?'

'Monday, the twenty-eighth. I am to take the steamship *Ferret* to Strome.'

'It's not long.'

'A fortnight this first Monday just.' She took my hand. 'Maybe I can get you a job, Calum Og, when I am down there.'

'Me?' I said, trying a laugh. 'I have a big enough job sorting things out here, never mind England.'

I had just finished a great feed of herring when Niall and Tormod Beag called for me. 'It is getting near the Sabbath, boy,' the *cailleach* warned, 'so don't you be gone long.'

We went over to the byre, and stood inside with the door open, the slow, heavy breathing of the cattle beasts enough to put me to sleep had I been on my own.

'Fearghus Mor was right enough,' Niall said. 'The tinkers are away. They were loading their carts when Tormod and me were bringing home the cattle.'

'Was the stranger along wi' them?' I asked.

'Aye, he was there,' Tormod Beag said. 'There is no mistaking him wi' that bright cloth he has at his neck. It was himself I saw go inside a tent; the only one still standing. All the others were down, ready for off.'

'He had some nerve,' Niall said, 'bringing that crowd down for fish. There was very near an army o' them.'

'Maybe he was only wanting his share,' I said.

'Away!' Tormod Beag scoffed. 'That crowd would ha' made off wi' your uncle's cart supposing they got the chance.'

'And loaded it to the gun'ales wi' herring,' Niall put in. 'It was hard lines, though, the monkey getting hit. Eachann Crubach was weeping, did you know that?'

'He had a great notion for the monkey,' I said.

'Fancy weeping over a beast,' Tormod Beag said. 'It was the stranger I was sorry for.'

I did not want to talk about Runag the monkey or Eachann Crubach weeping or the stranger, and I was glad when I heard Tormod Beag's mother calling him. 'I had best away,' he said, when enough time had passed to show that he was not scared of the *cailleach*.

I made no move to stop Niall when he went off with him, and I stood in the doorway of the byre watching them running between the corn stooks. There was a dark ring around the moon. As I closed the byre door, the rain started.

16

The rain was still coming down in the morning, falling that thick
the very air seemed to be descending in a mass of water upon the
earth. Sheets of water lay about the crofts; the corn stooks
sodden islands in a swelling sea. Even within the broad stone
walls of the house, with its thick roof of thatch, and the door tight
latched against the weather, the rain held dominion. It came
driving under the door, blackening the earthen floor, and
forming spreading pools; spilling down the wall as it seeped in at
the deep-set window; dripping steady through the thatch, and
hissing sharp on the fire. There was no daylight worth the name;
the fire flaming that bright at noon you would have thought the
day spent and it dusk. We had to have the lamp lit before supper
so that Tomas Caogach could see to read a passage from the
Book.

My chance to get clear of the house came after supper when
Tomas Caogach went off to bed, saying he was feeling his back
sore, and no wonder seeing the work he had put in at the shore
the day before. The *cailleach* was bent low on her stool, gazing
into the peat fire flames. She had taken to sitting still by the fire of
a Sabbath night, never once fidgeting — she who could not abide
her hands being idle — lost in a dreamy doze that always had her
dropping off to sleep where she sat.

The cattle were restless; I could hear them lowing in the byre.
'I had best put down dry bedding for the beasts,' I said, 'and take a
look at the corn stooks.'

She never lifted her eyes from the peat fire flames. I wondered
what she was seeing there. 'Hear the rain,' she said, swallowing a
yawn. 'You will get a soaking, boy.'

I waited until her head started to nod. In a little while, she
would be well away, although it was a wonder to me how she
could sleep like that and not fall off the stool. She murmured
something to herself, her lips twitching in a smile. On the other
side of the driftwood partition, Tomas Caogach let go a roarer of
a snore fit to rouse the dead. The *cailleach* never stirred. I got up
and went to the door and slowly eased up the latch.

I began to wonder if I was wise. It was worse than I had thought
now that I was outside the snug double walls of unhewn stone;

the rain sheeting down, the night loud with the sound of running water gurgling and gushing down every drain and water course, and at the back of it all the steady low rumble of the Rha falls in full spate. I put my head down, and ran for the byre.

By the time I reached the byre — and it not a score of strides from the house — there was not the breadth of a penny dry on me. I thought of turning back, but I had promised Marsali that I would keep her company, and she was bound to have a great feed waiting for me seeing she had the Lodge to herself. Standing in the deep doorway of the byre, I could not stop a shiver. There was a wind getting up, gusting in from the sea at the back of the flood tide, driving the rain into my face. It was a cold, hard rain. I would be soaked to the skin long before I reached the Lodge. Well, I was wet already, and there was nothing for me in the house but an early bed, and listening to Tomas Caogach's snores and the drip of the rain through the thatch. What decided me was the thought of getting my nose inside the Lodge and seeing the place for myself. I might be able to get Marsali to light the lamps in the big front room where the factor entertained the gentry. She said it was brighter than day with all the lamps lit, such a glare of light it was enough to blind you. That, and the thought of being able to slip through the big iron gates and walk the length of the drive, made me brave the rain. I had always wanted to pass through those fancy iron gates and march the length of the tree-lined drive, and I would never have another chance like this.

I ran up the path to the road, splashing through water that reached my ankles. I stopped at the road. The side drains were fast flowing streams, the road itself awash. Blinking the rain out of my eyes, I peered through the murk at the dark face of the hill. There was something wrong. The line of the hill seemed to have closed in on the road where the cut of the old quarry should have been. My eyes could have been deceiving me, but I had to find out. Putting my back to the Lodge, I went on up the road, slipping on gravel and mud as I advanced.

A great barrier of earth and stones was strewn across the road, near head high. There must have been a landslip. I jumped the flooded side drain, and scrambled up the slippery face of the hill, trying to see where the slide had started. The ground seemed to be quaking under my feet. I heard the roar first, felt the ground shake as if a heaving sea boiled beneath me, but I could not have moved to save my life. Ahead of me, the face of the hill broke open, and a great column of water spouted high in the air, spewing out stones and gravel along with it. Wet gravel showered down on me, stinging my face, and something struck me a glancing blow on the forehead. A rush of water swept my feet from under me, carrying me down the hill. I was swept across the road and over the bank on the other side. I remember thinking this was where I had once sent the Marag flying, and wondering if I would land in Mairi Beathag's midden, as I clawed feebly at the wet earth, vainly trying to halt my fall.

Something hard was digging into the small of my back. I had a moment of panic finding my feet higher than my head, wet black arms close to my eyes dripping down on my face, before I realised that I was wedged in a clump of rowans that grew near the bottom of the steep bank. It was the jagged stump of a broken branch that was digging into my back. I clawed myself up until I was on my knees, free of the rowan clump. It was when I raised my head to look up the bank that I heard the music.

There was no mistaking that queer, shrill music — no lilt to the tune at all — the thin, high notes sounding sharp above the beating of the rain and the noise of rushing water. The stranger was back, sending out the call on his silver whistle.

I scrambled up the bank on all fours, drawn by the thin thread of music, hearing its shrill call growing stronger, although the sound of a river in spate was loud in my ears. As I reached the road, another huge column of water gushed from the hill, tearing up whole banks of earth as it spouted forth. But the thread of music drew me on across the road, leading me away from the gushing water-spout to the dark outcrop of rock that marked the entrance to *Uamh an Oir* — a winking golden eye in the dark of the night.

I went up the face of the hill at a scrambling run, and I was at the opening of the cave before it came to me that no lightning had broken the dark of the rain-heavy sky to light that golden eye. But the sound of the stranger's music was too strong in my ears for me to hold back. I ducked inside the cave, bursting to greet him.

The cave was empty. The glittering walls lit a narrow bed of heather. That was all. The stranger was not there.

I stopped in the centre of the floor, gazing around in disbelief, hearing that queer, shrill music still, wondering how my ears could deceive me so. I had scanned the cave twice, and was searching the walls a third time before I spotted the narrow crack in the far corner, a crack so thin it was easy lost in the shadows. I wriggled through the narrow cleft in the rock until it widened into a funnel, screened by a thick bush of golden broom. I parted the branches and gazed out — gazed like one who has been blind from birth and suddenly has the dry, black scales peeled from his sightless eyes and sees the glory of the living world revealed for the first time.

I closed my eyes on the wonder before me, shut my ears to the call of the stranger's silver whistle, and edged my way back through the narrow cleft in the rock to the cave. I had to know why my eyes had been blind in the past; how I had missed the way until now, and the cave known to me all the days of my life. I looked around once more, satisfied that the thin, overlapping crack in the far corner would always have escaped me had the rock face not been glittering bright.

I squeezed through the opening again, and went down on my knees behind the broom. As I parted the branches, a flurry of golden blossom dropped into the water below, startling three speckled brown trout from their bed of white pebbles. The music had stopped, but I was not needing its queer, shrill call any longer.

The golden broom was on the bank of a stream that flowed through a broad glen; a beauty of a glen, a glen made for men who lived by the raising of their crops and cattle. I saw it all from behind the broom; the sun high in the sky shining down on the uplands and the broad flats of the arable. It was a green and smiling glen, a glen thick with trees and heavy with crops, full of fat cattle and sheep richly fleeced and all manner of birds.

I saw Seoras the dummy down by a pool, lying across the black mossy rocks under the green shade of spreading ferns, his head bent low to the stream where the water fretted and rippled over the stones; and I knew fine he was listening, Seoras, who had never before heard the sound of a stream flowing soft over stones or the rustle of ferns in the breeze or the hum of a bee. He got to his feet, as Eachann Crubach came leaping down the bank calling to him, Eachann with his crutches gone, his legs straight and true. The pair of them ran off rogether, Seoras singing like a lintie.

I was slow in picking out the stranger without the gaudy calico at his neck, his brown throat bare to the sun. He was sitting on a green bank above the stream where clusters of honeysuckle hung down to the water's edge, and a drooping willow sheltered chirping birds, idly rolling his silver whistle between his fingers.

He was watching Runag the monkey, who was watching Mata's pipe, and it going like a chimney. There was a broad shouldered man on the other side of the stranger, busy splicing a rope. He tossed back his straw coloured hair, and stared across at the broom. I thought he had spotted me, but I was too well hidden to be seen from the other bank, and it was a trout jumping in the pool that had caught his eye. His strong fingers went on working at the rope, and he turned to the stranger, and said, 'When is Calum Og coming?'

It was Mairi Beathag who answered him, and me not recognising her at first, clown that I was, just because she was out of her old rags, and had her wild white hair braided in a tidy pleat. 'He will not come without Marsali,' Mairi Beathag said, 'not Calum Og.'

'Aye, but there will be hard travelling for him,' Mata said, taking the pipe out of his mouth, and making a good spit, 'the road not easy, folks that blind they are not wanting to see the way.'

I did not see how that could be, but I was not for leaving Marsali behind. I got to my feet and squeezed through the narrow crack in the rock, and was out of the cave and slithering down the hillside, as if there were demons on my heels, I was that eager that Marsali should be the first to know the secret of the Cave of Gold.

I did not stop running until I reached the bridge over the Rha. It was the terrible roar of the falls that stopped me. The noise was enough to deafen you, enough — or so it seemed to my fearful ears — to shake the bridge from its moorings. Dark as it was, I could see the foaming torrent creaming under the bridge, hurtling down the deep, narrow gorge in its headlong rush to the sea. It was only the thought of the tidings I had for Marsali that got me across the bridge.

There was a rumbling roar ahead of me like the blast of a mighty cannon, and a grinding like that of a thousand giant harrows being raked across a rocky shore. I stopped again. The noise came from the Conon. I ran on down the road, past the open gates of the Lodge. I was rounding the bend by the Head Keeper's house, the river straight ahead, when the first flash of lightning lit the sky. But it was not the lightning that rooted me fast to the road.

The bridge over the Conon river was gone, swept away entire by a monstrous brownish yellow torrent that raged down from the hill. The stumps of two stone abutments on either bank stuck out like severed limbs. Thunder pealed over the hill; lightning raked the sky, that bright it tore apart the heavy curtain of rain. A tree came sweeping down on the flood, a hare crouched on the trunk, its bulging eyes starting from its head. The torrent had shifted the river from its old course, tearing through the sandy bank of the burial ground, and flattening the boundary wall of the Lodge, as it surged down to the sea.

As I watched — eyes bulging every bit as wide as those of the poor hare — a long, dark coffin slid slowly down the crumbling sandy bank and floated away, seized by the swirling water. The sight of that floating coffin brought me back to life. I ran back up the road, through the open gates of the Lodge, and down the long, tree-lined drive. I did not stop running until I plunged into the flood water around the house.

The Lodge was an island in the flood, the swollen river splitting into two foaming channels on either side of the house, as it met the flood tide that was breaking over the sea wall. The current tugged at my legs as the water rose above my knees. It was up to my waist when I slipped, and the kitchen wall near within reach. I scrabbled for a footing, stretched out for the looming wall, and was swept off my feet by the flood. My clawing fingers scraped on stone, fastened around a pipe, and clung to that pipe with a life of their own.

My feet found bottom, and dug in for a firm purchase to take the strain off my hands. Spitting water out of my mouth, I climbed the downpipe, and hauled myself on to the roof. The slates were treacherous, running with water, but Runag the monkey could not have clambered up to the skylight any faster. The light was closed, and I had to work my way up to the top of the long skylight, where I could get a grip on the raised lip. There was a lamp burning in the room. I hammered on the streaming glass with my free fist, and Marsali's frightened face peered up at me.

Her mouth opened wide. I could not hear for the roar of the flood, but she seemed to let out a shriek. For sure, my fist was sore beating on the glass before she stirred herself to lift the light on its slotted iron bar. Once she held it up, I slid down the roof, got my left hand in the gap, and seized the light in my right hand. 'Let go o' the bar,' I shouted, and flung the hinged light back on the roof. The glass shattered, but I was too busy getting my legs into the opening to worry about that. I dropped down into the room, bumped against the edge of the bed, and sat down heavily.

'Your head,' she gasped, staring at me as if I had sprouted horns. 'What have you done to your head?'

'I have seen wonders, Marsali,' I panted, breathless, but bent on getting the words out. 'I have seen Mata again, and him wi' his pipe going like a chimney, and Eachann Crubach wi' his legs made whole, and Seoras the dummy singing like a lintie, and himself hearing — Seoras *hearing*, Marsali — all o' them safe along wi' the stranger in a beauty of a secret glen at the back o' *Uamh an Oir*. You have got to come quick. I will show you.'

She started to weep! As sure as I am here, my sister Marsali started to weep! Sniffing back her tears, she snatched up a towel from the rail on the marble topped wash-stand, and held it gently against my head.

'What are you doing, girl?' I cried, pulling the towel away, and throwing it down on the bed.

She lifted a glass from a chest of drawers, and held it in front of my face. The chalk white face of a stranger glared back at me, hair plastered close to his scalp, a long, deep gash across the top of his forehead, streaming blood. I put a hand up to my head, and looked down stupidly at the blood on my fingers. 'I must ha' got a knock,' I said.

'You didn't know?'

'No, I never felt a thing. I thought the wet was the rain just.'

She dabbed her eyes with a corner of the towel, and handed it to me. 'Hold it tight against your head,' she commanded briskly, as if the tears had never been. 'I will get bandages.'

The house shook as something crashed against the gable end. There was the sound of breaking glass; the thud of something heavy falling. 'Be quiet, girl,' I said, seizing her arm. 'I must think.'

'Quiet?' she cried, near weeping again. 'I have been quiet all day here on my own, and all of a sudden the water bursting in at the door and flooding the kitchen and it dark then. The housekeeper went off first thing, and she has never come back.'

'She is stuck on the Cuil side. The bridge over the Conon is down.'

I did not fancy the way she was staring at me, as if it was a stranger before her, and one she was afraid of. But the look changed, and the talk came, the words fairly bubbling out. 'The water is everywhere,' she said, 'all over the bottom floor. I was looking out a front bedroom window just before you came, and

136

the tide is over the sea wall and up around the porch. What are we going to do?'

'Get out,' I said, 'before the whole house comes down.'

'The house cannot come down.'

'Can it not? The bridge over the Conon is down.'

'The house is different.'

'Old Seumas says the Lodge is built on sand, and it is a wonder it has not sunk long ago. The flood will not be long scouring away the sand. We have got to get out, and quick.'

'How?'

'The way I came in. It is easy enough, Marsali. You will manage fine wi' me along with you.'

She bit her lip, and tried a laugh. 'Well, I am not for staying on my own, I can tell you.'

'Ropes,' I said, thinking hard. 'We need ropes.'

She shook her head helplessly.

I looked down at the bed. 'We could try tearing up the blankets, and knotting them together.' But they would never reach, not for what I had in mind.

'Wait you,' Marsali said, 'the clothes lines. They are brought in from the washing green before the Sabbath.'

I made to get up, but she pushed me back on the bed, and handed me the towel again. 'Hold that against your head,' she said, more like the old, bossy Marsali, 'and keep it there.' She picked up the lamp from the chest of drawers. 'I will get the lines.'

After she had gone, I groped my way to the head of the narrow stair, listening to her splashing about below. The floor seemed to be moving under my feet, the timber joists groaning. There was a steady thudding noise outside above the roar of the flood. The torrent that had swept a stone bridge away must have rolled down great boulders from the hill. And the house stood in the path of all that the flood was carrying down to the sea. I was suddenly afraid for Marsali and shouted her name.

She came running up the stairs, her skirts wet to the waist. She was carrying a thick coil of fine white rope. I knotted an end around my waist, and slung the coil over my shoulder. 'Quick,' I said, bending my back under the sky-light opening. 'Up on my back, and on to the roof.'

She was tugging a drawer open; rummaging inside. 'I must get my papers,' she said, 'for the steamer and the railway.'

It was on my lips to tell her that she would forget them when she saw what lay beyond *Uamh an Oir*, but I kept my mouth shut. Time enough for that when we were clear of the Lodge. Marsali stuffed a linen envelope inside her bodice, and leapt lightly on to my back, and pulled herself up through the opening, nimble as any boy.

I followed her out on to the roof. The wind was up, gusting strong from the sea, lashing the rain down on us, and flinging clouds of spray over the house. I could taste the spray salt on my lips. I edged close to Marsali. 'Hold on tight,' I shouted above the roar of the surging waters, 'and wait till I come for you.'

It was easy enough sliding down the roof, and hanging from the gutter; no trouble getting my legs wedged around the downpipe, and sliding down that. But the moment I was into the water, the flood was greedy for my legs, and it was all I could do to stand fast as I worked the free end of the line behind the pipe and knotted it secure. I set my feet down hard, and made for the drive, leaning into the weight of the flood, paying out the line as I moved forward.

The water never came above my waist, except when I stumbled once or twice and it swirled around my chest, but the force of the flow was such that I could never have made the passage to dry ground unaided. It was Mairi Beathag who saved me. I could see her clear in my mind; Mairi Beathag — her old rags shed, her wild white hair braided in a tidy pleat — saying, '*He will not come without Marsali, not Calum Og.*'

It was her words that gave me the strength to endure, and I said them to myself when I felt the flood getting the better of me, and I kept on saying them, even when the water was down to my knees. I was still mumbling Mairi Beathag's words when I stumbled clear of the water and staggered towards the trees.

I was an age getting the wet knots undone, and the rope free from my waist. But I was not long in pulling it around the trunk of the nearest tree, drawing the line tight, and fastening it secure. The rest was easy. Going back holding tight to the line, climbing the downpipe once more, and guiding Marsali down.

But it was not easy for Marsali, that stiff with cold and fear she could scarce move, and she was more spent than I knew by the time we reached the shelter of the trees. When I said to her, 'We must go quick, and see the wonders beyond *Uamh an Oir*,' she gave a little moan, and fainted clean away. I caught her in my arms as she fell.

All the way along the road, arms linked tight, heads bent against the wind and the rain, I talked to Marsali, telling how I had been drawn to *Uamh an Oir*, and found the way to the green glen and witnessed the glory that was there. I had to shout against the noise of running water all around, and I could not tell if she was hearing me right. She did not utter a single word, only clutched my arm the tighter when I told of Seoras the dummy, his ear laid close to the murmuring stream, and Eachann Crubach leaping like a young deer.

We struggled on past the shoemaker's hut, past the merchant's shop, and me talking still, telling of the stranger and Runag and Mata, and the fair-haired man splicing rope, and Mairi Beathag. We passed the track leading down to our township — Marsali tugging at my arm, trying to lead me home, and myself keeping her going my way — until I saw that there was no way left to go.

I was struck dumb, not believing my eyes. But my eyes did not lie. I could not lead Marsali up the face of the hill to the Cave of Gold. The face of the hill had changed entire, wrought anew by a giant's hand. The outcrop of rock that marked the entrance to *Uamh an Oir* was gone, buried under a mountain of rocks and earth where a great mass of the hillside had come down upon it. Even the tail-end of the fall that had reached the road towered higher than the highest house in the place.

It was Marsali who saw the strip of coloured cloth flapping against a piece of wood that was caught between two boulders. She clambered up, and brought them down to me — the arm rest of a broken crutch, and a torn length of gaudy calico. I tossed the broken crutch away — Eachann Crubach was not needing it — and stuffed the cloth into my pocket.

17

Marsali did the talking, and kept it to what had gone on at the Lodge. When she was done, our mother gave me a hug, and clasped Marsali to her as if she would never let her go. Tomas Caogach was up and dressed, roused from his bed by the *cailleach* when I had failed to return from the byre. 'You did well, boy,' he said; and he was the one who got me dry clothes, while our mother attended to Marsali, and it was himself who bound the wound in my head with a length of clean cloth.

'I am not caring supposing the corn ends up in the bay,' the *cailleach* declared, that flushed and happy-looking you would have thought it was good news we had brought home. 'We never died a winter yet, and many a bad one we came through. Good grief, the two o' you could have perished, easy. Put your feet to the fire, and warm them, girl.'

She bustled around, brewing tea and setting out scones, chattering away all the time, and Marsali was not slow to see that her time had come. She read them the letter from the laird's cousin, and the pair of them were all approving nods and smiles, for a wonder. And when she showed them the papers that would take her on the steamer and the railway, they handled them with such care you would have thought they were afraid the papers might crumble into dust at their touch.

What talk was on the go, the three of them going at it good style. I sat quiet, feeling the crumpled ball of gaudy calico in my pocket, trying to work out why the way had been barred to me. '*There will be hard travelling for him,*' Mata had said, '*the road not easy, folk that blind they are not wanting to see the way.*' And it came to me, sitting quiet in the kitchen, deaf to the clatter of tongues, why the way had been barred to me. My travelling was not done. I had been left behind to show others the way. The stranger had let me see the end of the road, so that I was armoured against all doubt, no matter how hard the travelling. He had taken only those who were too heavy laden — Mairi Beathag, Seoras the dummy, Eachann Crubach — and lifted their burdens clean from them, as easy as the wind shakes free a puff of thistle-down.

But why had he left Coinneach Beag chained to his bed, himself not able to lift his head from his pallet unaided? He must have taken Coinneach. I had not stayed long enough, hidden behind the golden broom, to see if he was a part of the company. I had gone rushing off for Marsali, never giving poor Coinneach a thought. But he must be there, safe with the stranger and the rest of the company.

'You should get to your bed, boy,' the *cailleach* said.'It is a good sleep you are needing after that knock on the head.'

'I am fine,' I said, looking up to see the three of them with their eyes latched fast on my face, wondering how long they had been watching me on the sly.

'Boil another pot o' tea, Iseabal,' Tomas Caogach said. 'It will soon be dawn, and we will see what is to be done.'

Nothing could be done about the Lodge, that was easy seen, even in the faint first light of day. All that was left standing was the stump of a gable end, poking a thick finger through the swollen river, as it surged over the breached sea wall into the loch; a loch whose muddy waters bore the wreckage of the flood. Most of our corn was gone, only a few battered sheaves remaining where the land was not under water. The cattle were lowing loud in the byres, something I had never heard before at this time of day.

Every house in the township had a cluster of watchers at the door; every house save Mairi Beathag's. And every eye was drawn to the bare gap where the Lodge had stood. Not a one of them looked back at the hill, only Marsali and myself gazed up at the long black scar where the landslip had stripped the face of the hill bare to the rock.

Fearghus Mor and Raonull came squelching round the end of the house. 'What a fall there has been on the hill,' Fearghus Mor cried. 'The spur above *Uamh an Oir* is deep down under a mountain o' rubble, and the fall slid right down to the road. It will be days before the mail-coach manages through to Staffin. But there is one blessing in it; all them that are able will get work clearing the road.'

Raonull was gazing around at the watchers. 'Whoever saw near everyone in the place out o' their bed at this time o' day before?' he said.

'There are some in this place would not rise from their beds at the crack o' dawn,' Fearghus Mor said. 'Old Mairi Beathag is not out. The old witch is sleeping still.'

'Not here,' I said. 'She is safe wi' the stranger at the back of *Uamh an Oir*, free o' your mocking.'

They looked at me as if I had taken leave of my senses, all except Marsali. Tomas Caogach tapped his head. 'The boy got a bad knock last night,' he said, 'pulling Marsali out o' the Lodge. It was no easy job, I am telling you. Calum Og did well, but he got a bad knock.'

'That boy is forever dreaming,' Fearghus Mor growled, 'knock on the head or no knock on the head. Mooning around dreaming, that is what is wrong wi' him. Many's the time he is not even hearing what is said to him he is that far gone in his dreams.'

'Cry Mairi Beathag,' I said, surprising myself, I was that calm with him, not wild at all. 'Cry Seoras the dummy. Cry Eachann Crubach. Cry Coinneach Beag. See if any o' them come to your call. They are away wi' the stranger beyond *Uamh an Oir*, Seoras the dummy wi' a tongue on him and ears to hear, Eachann Crubach wi' his legs made whole, Coinneach Beag — .'

'Is it a seer you think you are?' Fearghus Mor roared. He turned to the others. 'Did you ever hear the like? A beardless boy making out he is seeing visions.'

'Cry them by name,' I said, 'and see if they come to your call.' I turned my back on him, and walked into the house.

Marsali and the *cailleach* followed me inside, our mother wringing her hands. 'Why must you vex them so wi' your stories?' she said. 'You know fine Fearghus Mor creates at the least thing. You will have him making mock o' you all over the township.'

'Not if the four o' them are gone,' Marsali said slowly, her dark eyes fast on my face.

Tomas Caogach led the way into the kitchen, Fearghus Mor by his side, and a host gathered at their back, crowding the room to the door. They were all looking at me as if a stranger had come among them, and themselves unaware of his approach. Tomas Caogach cleared his throat, and bent down to me. 'Is it the second sight you have, Calum Og?' he whispered.

'He did not see Coinneach Beag,' Fearghus Mor boomed. 'Coinneach Beag is safe in his bed.'

'Aye, but the other three,' Raonull gulped, plucking at his beard, 'the other three.'

'No,' I said.

Every eye in the room was upon me; Dughall, the father of Coinneach Beag, straining to see over Fearghus Mor's broad shoulder.

'No,' I said, 'Coinneach Beag cannot be in his bed.'

Tomas Caogach looked at Fearghus Mor, but the big fellow was silent for once. 'The other three are gone,' he said, 'but Coinneach Beag lies in his bed.'

I got to my feet, and the crowd parted before me, as I made for the door. I knew fine they were close at my back, but I did not once look round all the way to the house, and it the very last one, at the far end of the township. I had my hand on the latch of the door when Dughall seized my arm. 'What are you going to do to Coinneach?' he said, that fearful you would have thought I was armed for war.

'Speak to him,' I said.

He nodded, staring at me as if I was a stranger, and he must take in the lineaments of my face so that he would know me again. 'I will keep the rest o' them out,' he said. 'Coinneach would take a scare if they all crowded in, and he is not fit for it.'

Coinneach Beag was lying in the box-bed in the kitchen. Not even the glow of the peat fire flames could warm the white of his thin face. The bed looked too big for him. I knelt on the floor, gripping the wooden frame of the bed. 'Were you sleeping last night, Coinneach,' I asked him, 'when the flood came?'

'No, I was listening to the rush o' water,' he said.

'Did you not hear the stranger calling?' I said, 'playing that queer tune o' his on his silver whistle?'

'How could I be hearing, Calum Og?' he said, 'and me in bed and ours the end house in the township? I never get to hear anything lying here.'

'You must ha' heard,' I said, 'and the notes that shrill they would ha' pierced a head o' stone.'

'The noise o' the flood was that loud,' he said, 'I was not hearing anything but the water. Wait you,' he said, and his eyes brightened, 'I did hear a queer, shrill kind o' cry. But I thought it was a bird caught by the flood.'

'Why did you not rise from your bed?' I said. 'Coinneach Beag, why did you not rise from your bed?'

'I am not able,' he said. 'You know I am not able.'

I took hold of his hands. 'Listen,' I said, 'and I will tell you what I have seen. Last night Seoras the dummy answered the call of the stranger, and it took him to *Uamh an Oir*, and beyond the cave into a glen — you never saw such a glen, Coinneach — thick with cattle wi' bellies on them like barrels, and a shine on their coats better than your father's best boots on the Sabbath. And

Seoras had the use of his ears, Seoras could hear the softest sound — hear the purl of a stream rippling slow over stones — and I heard him sing, Seoras the dummy, sing. And Eachann Crubach; Eachann heard the call, and came to the cave, and cast away his crutches, and I saw him with his legs made straight, leaping like a deer. You should ha' gone, Coinneach. You should ha' risen from your bed. What kept you back?'

'I am not able,' he cried, near weeping. 'I am not able.'

'Did you have to see him first?' I said, wild with him. 'Was his music not enough to draw you from your bed? Did you have to see him wi' this about his throat?' and I let go of his hands, and took the ball of gaudy calico from my pocket and unfurled it. The coloured cloth streamed across the bed like a banner.

Coinneach Beag sat up. 'I am not able, Calum Og,' he said.

I got to my feet. 'You are sitting up, Coinneach,' I said. 'For any favour, boy, you can walk.'

He pushed the blankets away, and swung his thin legs out from the bed. I laid my hands on his knees. His legs were freezing cold to the touch, but there was sweat on his face. 'Up you get, Coinneach,' I said. 'Up you get and walk out o' the house along wi' me.'

'I will fall,' he said. 'I will fall if I stand.'

But he was raising himself from the bed; standing upright. His hands reached out for me. I backed away. He came after me — slowly, slowly. slowly, but he came, taking short steps, his stride no longer than a hen's, stepping slow across the floor. He walked. Coinneach Beag walked.

I got the door open, and backed out, and he came after me. But it was not me he was looking at now — it was his father and mother; the two of them clutching hands, as they watched Coinneach Beag, taking his slow, short steps, walk towards them.

A long, slow breath escaped from the crowd, and Coinneach Beag's glad shout, 'I can walk!' was drowned in a sudden clamour of voices.

I walked away, bone weary all of a sudden, my head starting to ache bad. All I wanted to do was to lie down and let sleep splice together all the ragged thoughts that chased through my mind. I thought of the fair-haired man, who had asked the stranger when I was coming, wondering why I had been so slow in seeing who he was, and himself busy splicing a rope, and that the job of a seafaring man.

144

Marsali caught up with me. 'I have been thinking, Calum Og,' she said, that breathless she could hardly get the words out. 'The man you saw along wi' the stranger — the one wi' hair like straw, who asked about you — I know who he was.'

I sang dumb, and let her tell me. It was better that way.

MASTER OF MORGANA
Allan Campbell McLean

Niall is convinced that his brother's near fatal fall was
no accident. Someone wanted Ruairidh to die when he
fell into the deep gorge. But who would want to kill
quiet and kind Ruairidh?

Against everyone's advice, but determined to solve
the mystery, Niall takes Ruairidh's place on the fishing
crew. His search for the truth leads Niall into a web of
intrigue and suspicion, and suddenly he realises that
he too could be in terrible danger...

Set against the lonely and rugged background of Skye
this is a vivid and thoroughly gripping story.

'Quite unlaydownable'. *The Scotsman*

'McLean writes like John Buchan at his best. You just
cannot put it down.' *Times Literary Supplement*

ISBN 0 86241 275 7   £3.50 pbk

RIBBON OF FIRE
Allan Campbell McLean

Skye, 1884. The population, greatly depleted during the Highland Clearances, is still suffering from thoughtless landlords and greedy factors.

Young Alasdair Stewart finds himself caught up in the rebellious activities of the menfolk and he very soon has to bear the consequences.

But how are their most secret plans constantly forestalled? Is there a traitor in their midst? And the landlord with his proud and spirited daughter, do they too not want peace and prosperity for the land?

Beyond the reach of the militia, hidden for days in the remotest part of the island, this desperate band see no hope for their land or their future...

'A beautiful, memorable, stirring book...'
Times Literary Supplement

'From the moment of the capture of Alasdair, the story piles up into a rhythm of epic excitement.'
The Scotsman

ISBN 0 86241 074 6   £2.99 pbk

A SOUND OF TRUMPETS
Allan Campbell McLean

In the exciting sequel to *Ribbon of Fire*, the laird's tyrannical successors create unrest for the islanders once more. Alasdair Stewart is forbidden his promised education and is forced to work in another part of the island. Here he learns of some new treachery against his own people.

Tension builds as resistance to this news mounts—burnt hayricks, a smashed beer-cellar, the accidental death of one of the landlord's men—all further excuses to bring these rebellious islanders to heel. Lachlan Ban promises to find a way to avoid meeting their extortionate demands and a daring plot is hatched.

In the hair-raising adventures that follow, we see once again this master story-teller at his fighting best. Is escape possible? Is exile inevitable?

ISBN 0 86241 095 9   £2.99 pbk

THE HILL OF THE RED FOX
Allan Campbell McLean

'Unknown man found shot,' said the newspaper head-line. Alasdair recognised the man he had met on the train to Skye, the man who had slipped him a desperate last message 'Hunt at the Hill of the Red Fox M15'.

Alasdair finds the Hill of the Red Fox on Skye, but the note still makes no sense. Nor at first do most of the strange and dangerous goings on on the island, many of which involve Alasdair's sinister uncle, Murdo Beaton. There is much more than the odd bit of poach-ing happening—atomic scientists and their secrets are disappearing.

People are not always what they seem. Whom can Alasdair really trust? In finding out he uncovers a web of espionage—and all its perils!

ISBN 0 86241 055 X   £3.50 pbk

02 0 39002443

CANONGATE SILKIES

Silkies are human on land, but in water they transform themselves into seals. Canongate Silkies is a new series incorporating folk tales, short stories and poetry that reflects the ancient magic of the Seal People.

THE BROONIE, SILKIES AND FAIRIES
Duncan Williamson

Master storyteller Duncan Williamson vividly retells the timeless travellers' tales of the magical beings of the Otherworld: the testing Broonie; the, elusive Silkies; and the mischievous Fairies of the summer hills.
ISBN 0 86241 456 3   £3.50 pbk

FIRESIDE TALES
Duncan Williamson

On cold winter nights when darkness enclosed the traveller's camp, a father would sit his children down and tell a story. A collection of twelve such folk and fairy tales, entertaining, scary, funny and clever.
ISBN 0 86241 457 1   £3.50 pbk

THE WELL AT THE WORLD'S END
Norah and William Montgomerie

Thirty five folktales, legends and some poems, from almost every corner of Scotland: Celtic legends; animal fables; fairy tales of mermaids, ogres and princesses. For tellers, readers and listeners of stories everywhere.
ISBN 0 86241 462 8   £3.50 pbk

IN

01599
511
407
_____

01599534
(KYLE)   161
    ___